KINGDOM

OF

SECRETS

KINGDOM

OF

SECRETS

J. A. GARTH

ISBN: 978-0-6488095-8-6

Social Media:

FACEBOOK:

https://www.facebook.com/j.ann.author/

TWITTER:

https://twitter.com/JessicaAauthor

INSTAGRAM:

instagram.com/j.a.garth_author/

For Nigel, Jeanette and Lillian,

It takes a village to create a world, and I'm grateful I've got you in mine.

CHAPTER ONE

The sun's golden rays had broken through the trees surrounding the kingdom long after Aedlin Malheim had woken up absolutely sure of one thing — at noon today, an entire kingdom would be attending the funeral of the wrong fae. Because of that, her life is never going to look the same.

She sits on the end of her bed and stares at the black gown that hangs innocently on the hook by her wardrobe, unsuspecting of her desire to grab the closest pair of scissors in her reach and destroy every last thread. She wonders if there would be a mad rush to find her a replacement gown or if she will be given permission to stay in bed all day. It's a ridiculous thing for her to consider, of course. So, with a clench of her fists so tight her nails dig into her palms she does her best to accept the inevitable. She releases her tight grasp, gets to her feet, and puts on the most hated garment she's even had to wear and with it, everything it represents.

After today, she is expected to forget everything about herself, her wants, needs, and desires and become a perfect copy of her mother. It's her turn to become Malheim's next Queen, and the very thought sends her into a panic. Aedlin throws her head back. She wants to cry out; she wants to force out the fear and anxiety that is drowning her and run away from it all, but it's just another stupid idea, where could she possibly run to? Her mind is in shambles as it battles itself with her dilemma. What does she know of running a kingdom? Sure, she had been groomed for this her whole life, hell she was born for it, but she was never supposed to be thrown into the deep end like this.

Years of preparing still doesn't feel like enough and for this very reason, she can't possibly begin to understand why her mother would be the one to fall terminally ill, rather than her. Aedlin's mother was someone who had the experience to continue her role as Queen of Malheim. She is—was graceful, knowledgeable and was given more time before it was expected of her to take her place on the throne. As opposed to Aedlin, an inexperienced, *barely* reached adulthood fae who had to recently surrendered a pet fish to one of the local children because she could hardly remember to feed it.

The orange glow from the flames that flicker in the fireplace dance across Aedlin's tear-stained face. She has cried so much over the last three days, partly because of the grief of losing her mother but also, in large part, because of the suffocating panic she has felt since she held her mother's hand as she took her final breath. And now, on the morning of Queen Frayett's funeral, there seems to be nothing left besides a few tears that fall sparingly. The reality of Aedlin's life going forward without her mother is a weight she knows she isn't ready for, despite being shaped into who she is needed to be.

Everyone, especially Aedlin's mother, was sure she had finally become ready to be crowned Queen as the end of her life drew nearer. But Aedlin knew better, even if she didn't *dare* tell her mother such thoughts. The faefolk of Malheim don't need a shadow of Frayett—Queen of Malheim, they need *her*. Even if the majority of Queen Frayett's time had been spent continuing to do just as her own parents had - hide all of them away from the erst of Agoura rather than allowing them to fight for their rightful place among the others who surround their kingdoms limits.

Today everyone is expected to honour and celebrate Queen Frayett's life but not one single soul is ready for that. No, today will be heavy with the weight of her loss, but not the acceptance of it.

Aedlin crosses her bedroom slowly to the open window needing some fresh air. She makes sure to not let herself trip over the bottom of her hand sewn floor length gown made and designed specifically for today's occasion at the request of Aedlin's mother.

The hairs on the back of her neck stand on end as she watches the trees that line the kingdom sway gently, the breeze they are carrying caresses the exposed parts of her skin but even *it* seems to be grieving the loss of the Queen. Aedlin reminisces fondly about one of the tales her mother told her growing up of the magic they hold, not just in their kingdom but it's surroundings and how everything around them, from each single blade of grass to the clouds that float lazily above have the heart of our ancestors within and when we grieve, so too, do they.

The breeze that would usually carry along the scent from the wildflowers that grow in the otherwise empty fields just within the perimeter is eerily empty.

The kingdom below is still a bustle with morning chores to complete and preparations for today's event are being carried out but it's all wrong, as if Queen Frayett took all of the happiness, music and magic that Malheim is usually rich with, with her.

The door to Aedlin's room opens slowly behind her. She doesn't bother turning to see who has entered without knocking, she already knows, besides her mother there is only one other whoever freely enters her rooms without permission.

"I'm not ready for this Melody." Aedlin whispers, openly confessing to her, just as she always has.

"For today or what is expected of you after?" Melody asks, placing a symptomatic hand on Aedlin's shoulder. Her grip is firm, but not painful, although, Aedlin has a pretty good idea of just how painful it could be. Her mother had decided against using the usual choices for a nanny, like a teacher or a healing fae. Instead, she requested a warrior. Someone who could be strict, disciplined, driven but above all else, they would protect her child against any and all odds put against them.

Melody quickly became an obvious choice for Aedlin's mother. She saw that there was more in her heart than just a drive to protect. That was the magic she had been blessed with, the ability to see the truth in other's hearts and the true nature of their intentions. She saw Melody's ability to nurture, and just as Aedlin's mother had expected, Melody took on her new role. She prioritised a dedicated amount of time every day to keeping up with her training, and other parts of her spare time were spent with other fae around Malheim to learn how best to care for a child. She became Aedlin's teacher, tended to her wounds with care and patience and after some time began giving her the same training she herself had been taught. This is something that Aedlin hated at first. Trying to learn a fae talent that is not the one you are born with is brutal. Every fibre within you knows that what you're doing is not right. What would have taken a natural—born warrior fae weeks at most took Aedlin months. By the time she was sixteen, she could finally do most of what warrior fae could do by fourteen.

"Both," Aedlin whispers, not knowing if Melody heard.

"Aedlin, turn around."

Reluctantly, Aedlin turns to face her. Melody's eyes are puffy and red. Her usually wild, sandy blonde curls are pulled back into a sensible bun and she is wearing one of Aedlin's mothers sleeved, floor length black gowns. Aedlin forces herself to focus on Melody's green eyes. She knew that her mother had picked out a gown for Melody to wear because she didn't own anything funeral appropriate of her own, as much as Melody had protested. Aedlin is glad that in the end, despite her protests, Melody decided to wear it, but she hadn't expected how much seeing her wear it would make her feel like breaking down all over again.

"You are all that Malheim has left. Now that your

mother is gone, they need someone to lead them, they need direction—security and someone to keep them and their homes peaceful and free from the dangers that surround our kingdom's limits. *You* are who they need."

"I'm not..." Aedlin begins, but Melody puts her hands up, signalling for her to stop.

"I know you don't think you're ready. I know you think you can't fill the shoes of your mother. But what you fail to see, you usually so clever girl, is that no one, not even your mother, expects you to rule just as she did. Do you really think she followed her parents' footsteps exactly as they laid them? Absolutely not, not only did she know you would do her job differently, but she also hoped you would."

Aedlin considers for a fleeting moment asking about her father, it should at least be considered that there is an attempt to locate her father and allow him to take his rightful place as king, he is, after all, her mother's husband. Making him the rightful King of Malheim. The narrowing of Melody's field green eyes and the flicker of warning to stop pushes Aedlin's unspoken suggestion somewhere deep down. Where the questions she has about her father usually go. Through her nineteen years all that she has learned about her father is that his and her mother's love was fierce, intense and dangerous. For some reason, her mother saw no reason for her to know more beyond that.

"Will you help me through this?" Aedlin asks quietly.

"Aedlin, I will be right by your side, just as I always have been, just as I always will be."

"You have always done far more than is expected of you Melody. You are more than I deserve."

"Oh, my sweet child." Her narrowed eyes soften, and she gives a sad smile. "Raising you has been worth every moment of my time and every ounce of love I have within me. I never did more than I expected of myself to raise you into the beautiful, strong, intelligent fae you have grown to be, just as your mother had hoped. Just as I had too." Melody reaches out and Aedlin instinctively steps closer to her. She re-pins one of Aedlin's raven-coloured curls that had fallen loose.

"I'm afraid we have no time left to delay; you are needed downstairs to go through one final rehearsal for today."

Aedlin sighs and turns back to the window and continues watching the fae below.

"I hate that all of this is so scripted, it doesn't feel right. I want to talk about the things my mother did that made me proud, that made me love her and that I will miss about her. I don't want lines created by someone else, as if they were my own."

"Please stop being difficult. I just need you to hold

your head up for a few hours."

Aedlin shakes her head and scoffs.

"Excuse me?" she says, Aedlin can practically hear Melody's eyebrow raise.

"I won't be doing as I'm told for a few hours. This is what the rest of my life will look like. I watched my mother work. From the moment I could make my way around this wretched castle, I watched her rule. But it wasn't really her ruling a thing, was it, Melody?" Aedlin crosses her arms.

"Everything your mother did was to protect you and everyone else in Malheim. Perhaps you are right, perhaps you are not ready to fill the shoes of your mother. A fae who put the protection of her people above all else, not because she was forced to, but because the love of her people drove her to decide what was best."

"I'm sorry. I don't know what's come over me." Aedlin says with a frown. The truth is, unfortunately, she knew exactly what has come over her, but just as she always has, she distracts and redirects, shielding what she's feeling inside. Aedlin knew she should have known better than to allow herself to have such a dramatic outburst. She knew her mother well and although she did not agree with the way that she ran the kingdom and although she feels trapped within not just the protective walls hugging the fae within its boundaries but also the walls within the castle, she knows what she has always known—her mother did everything she did to protect those she loved and as Melody had said, that was every one of her people, especially Aedlin.

"I know you are." Melody replies, but there is something missing in her tone.

"Look, we can continue to stand here and argue, or we can go down and let your mother go with some dignity and you can do the one thing that she has requested of you. After that, although you are still my responsibility to care for—you have every right to dismiss me of my duties. If you wish for me to stop pestering you about what it is your mother wanted for you, then that's probably the best option for you to proceed with."

Aedlin's mouth falls open in shock and she gasps. She knew that things could get heated between them sometimes. Usually, they both just yell and scream until they've said what is needed, then forgive and forget. Never before has she threatened to walk away from Aedlin or given her the option to walk away from her.

"Melody, you have always been like a second mother to me. I've just lost my first one I have no desire to lose the other. Besides, the only chance I stand at getting through any of this is by having you by my side." Aedlin barely manages to keep her composure together.

"If you truly believe that then you will make your way

downstairs immediately and get this over and done with so we can move on from today and the pain it holds and get started on what this kingdom needs from you."

Aedlin's stomach knots and her heart muscles strain. She almost gasps in pain but shields it from Melody. She needs her to trust that she will be there when Melody needs her to be. But first, she needs a moment to compose herself to be able to hold her head high and face what is waiting for her downstairs.

"I promise to be right down. Please, go ahead of me and let the royal advisor know to expect me within a few moments."

Melody looks at Aedlin wearily but thankfully gives ger a small nod before leaving her room and leaving her alone.

Aedlin wraps her hand tight around the necklace that sits against her chest. Of all the gifts her mother had ever given her this single necklace has always been the most meaningful, and not just because she had always made sure to remind her to never remove it or because she had had it blessed to always keep her safe from harm – but because it's delicate swirls of silver that match the shape of Aedlin's wings now hold a much sadder place in her heart. She had only recently realised she had never thanked her mother for it. The part of her mother she has left, that she gifted Aedlin the day she was born and was used as a means to keep her safe feels heavier now with the weight of knowing she will never get the chance to thank her like she should have.

She doesn't have the time to dwell on it now, she will have the rest of her life to regret what she did and didn't do with and for her mother.

Aedlin gives the silver wings one final squeeze before finally working up the courage to leave her rooms.

She doesn't allow herself to lock eyes with any of the other fae she passes throughout the halls of the castle. She couldn't stand to see their sad eyes matching that of her own. Part of her feels like she should have half a mind to lose it at every single one of them. How could they grieve just as she is for a mother that wasn't even theirs? How could their cries of distress at the discovery of her mother's death fill the walls of the castle – the very limits of this kingdom as if they all felt the same as her? But truthfully, she knew why, because to them, she was their mother. For the last forty years she has nurtured this kingdom. They mourn Aedlin's dead mother because she was their mother too.

After three flights of stairs and a few too many mumbles of "I'm sorry for your loss's." Aedlin finally makes it to the long table room to the right of the grand foyer where the Queen's advisor Dareyth is waiting.

With one final broken inhale, Aedlin pushes the doors open. Situated in the centre of the room is the comically large table that was used by Aedlin's mother and her grandparents whenever there was something of great importance to be discussed or debated. The queen's advisor is sitting at the far end of the table where Aedlin's mother would usually sit and where she should now be. He has his head held high and proud, and it makes Aedlin want to punch him right between his pointed chin and thin nose.

Aedlin looks at Melody questioningly. Melody shakes her head, silently telling her to let it go. By some miracle, Aedlin manages to force down the rage that is building hot and heavy throughout her body and takes a seat to his right, across from Melody, facing her.

"It is nice of you to finally decide to free up enough time to join us today." He says with a voice that is almost snake-like and nothing like Aedlin had ever heard him sound like before. Aedlin had never particularly liked him. Nor had she ever understood what his reasons were for needing to stalk around the walls of the castle at all hours. He had his own home and his own office outside of the castle. The only fae who lived in the castle who were not her mother or herself were Melody and the guards. Everyone else, cooks, cleaners, seamstresses and everyone in between who had anything to do with the castle had their own homes. Yet, no matter what time of day or night, Aedlin was almost guaranteed to spot him around the castle. On more than one occasion, he she had spotted him in passing while sneaking to the kitchen to sneak some late-night treats. But even still, even with Aedlin not liking something about him, it's never sat quite so thick between them as it is now. There is a darkness to his eyes that wasn't there before and the way his voice sounds makes an icy shiver run throughout Aedlin's spine.

Melody throws another warning look in Aedlin's direction. This one is as sharp as a dagger, but this time, she refuses to entertain Melody's silent threat.

"Please excuse my inconsideration for your time Dareyth, I should have known to be more respectful of you. I assure you, prioritising the grief I am feeling for the loss of my mother will not take up any more of your obviously very precious time."

Aedlin bows her head, shielding her smile from Melody. When she looks up again, she can almost feel Melody's anger vibrating across the table.

"There is no place in this castle for your smart mouth and childish behaviours Aedlin. Not anymore. Your mother may have tolerated it, but only because she couldn't see beyond you being her daughter. It made her lose sight of the future you would inevitably end up with and how she should have prepared you better, sooner, rather than allowing you to run the castle walls free to do as you pleased."

"My mother did the best she could. She gave me the best she had." Aedlin says, waving her hand toward Melody.

"Even so, you are yet to learn how to not speak out of turn. Then again, what am I to expect with a father like yours? He might not have made a physical impact on the way you were raised, but genetics are a powerful thing and clearly, as I unfortunately expected, you have ended up with his most undesirable traits."

Lava, actual molten lava replaces the blood that was coursing through Aedlin's body. Her cheeks heat with the words that fill her mouth, threatening to fall from the tip of her tongue in the form of word vomit all over Dareyth. Aedlin's lips part slowly in anticipation for the angry wrath she is about to throw at him, but she doesn't get the chance to say a thing. Melody is out of her seat and has her hand braced on the long sword that Aedlin hadn't noticed Melody had obviously taken off and placed beside her at the table.

"Melody?" This time it's Aedlin's time to warn her against her actions.

Melody ignores Aedlin completely and without breaking eye contact with Dareyth begins slowly and purposefully removing her sword from its scabbard. Her hand tightens around the black and gold hilt turning her knuckles white under the pressure.

Aedlin is *mostly* sure Melody wouldn't *actually* attack Dareyth. She has always been the most level-headed of the lot of them. Of course, with her mother's funeral today, it would be forgivable for her to not completely have her wits about her. She hasn't exactly hidden the stress of today. Perhaps Aedlin's mothers' death is the one thing that could finally break her. Aedlin finds it almost tempting to let Melody do as she wishes to Dareyth. He is keeping his demeanour as poised as he possibly can, but his fear is still visible in the widening of his eyes and the way he is chewing the inside of his cheek.

Melody's sword is halfway out of the scabbard with no sign of her hesitating with the decision she is making. The realisation that Melody is *actually* going to do it snaps Aedlin back to reality enough for her to acknowledge the consequences.

"Melody, you're excused." Surprisingly Aedlin's words stop Melody in her place, but she doesn't show any signs of wanting to move.

"Now, Melody."

She slides the sword back in its place, picks it up from the table and without a word leaves the room.

"You're not Queen yet Aedlin, you might want to calm down with throwing around demands as if you're actually in charge of anyone." Dareyth says as he wipes his hands over the front of his white robe, straightening it back out then takes his place back in Aedlin's mother's seat.

"I would think, considering I just saved your life you would show me a little more gratitude." Aedlin raises her eyebrow. "I have no desire to have anyone answer my command. Especially Melody. It was *only* because I was not willing to have blood spilled in my home on this day of farewell and celebration that I sent her out."

A smile creeps to the edges of Dareyth's lips and he shakes his head slowly, making his black hair become a little dishevelled.

"Please, she wouldn't have dared lay her blade against me. She knows she would find herself kicked out of the castle and without the protection of the Queen's guard, perhaps she would even find herself kicked out of the kingdom."

Aedlin positions herself in Dareyth. She squares her shoulders and stares at him until she can see from the twitch in his eye that she is pissing him off.

"On who's authority? Because there is nothing, she could do that would make me, the only one who has the authority to make that decision, send her away. Not even if it was your life she ended." Aedlin snarls through clenched teeth.

"You have a lot to learn about the reality of the position you stand to hold and just how little of a contribution you will truly get to make. If you thought your mother had no real position of power you will soon learn that compared to you, she actually had the job everyone believed her to have."

The fire bubbling through Aedlin's chest becomes unbearable. Who *is* he? Had he treated her mother the very same way? Perhaps that's why she never allowed Aedlin to question why he was always here in the castle.

"We will see just how long that lasts. I don't care what it takes, but things around here are going to change. Starting with you and the throne you seemed to have put yourself on."

He lets out a low chuckle. "You mean the throne your grandparents put me on? If your mother hadn't gone and given herself up to a dark elf like some common filthy, street whore then in doing so, creating you, they never would have lost trust in you mothers judgement and in turn decided that in the best interest of everyone that I be appointed the very important job of overseeing every. Single. Decision your mother—and now you — make."

Aedlin's hand flies through the air toward his face and before she can blink, her hand connects with Dareyth's cheek. The realisation of what she has just done comes faster than the sting on her hand. Her feet move before she wills them too, and within seconds, she has left the high priest with a satisfied smirk and is sprinting through the castle, trying to find Melody. She decides to begin with her sleeping quarters. She takes the stairs two at a time, almost tripping over her dress every other step. She rushes down the west wing until she reaches Melody's room and knocks on the door, but the housekeeper who passes informs Aedlin that Melody hasn't been back there since early this morning.

"I know she tends to use the courtyard when she's trying to take a moment to herself and if you don't know where she is, I would say it's a safe bet she's there, especially today." The housekeeper says, then gives Aedlin a sympathetic smile.

Aedlin gives her a nod and hurries out to the courtyard, tripping herself up twice as her mind races, distracted with the high priest's revelation about her father. She considers briefly that he is lying, but something tells her she knows he isn't.

She finally reaches the courtyard to see Melody sitting on a bench under the towering elder tree that for generations has sat in this exact spot with its wide, dark green leaves showering over its wide trunk. The hidden location of the tree, known only by certain members of the fae – kind was how her grandparents knew that where it has always stood in the hidden forest would be the perfect location for them to keep everyone hidden away and safe, and so, very quickly Malheim was built. Aedlin looks up at the tree and her shoulders drop. It seems more and more of the tree is unseasonably dying off every day. Just another thing added to the list that is very much about to become her problem to solve. But first, she needs to deal with confronting Melody for keeping such an enormous secret from her for her entire life. Her heart hammers and her hands tremble as the anger builds. How could she keep something so huge from her? how could Aedlin ever trust her again? It's completely reasonable to expect that her mother would have secrets with Melody that she would want kept from Aedlin, but how could she look at Aedlin every time she had ever asked her about her father and blatantly lie? Worse than that, how could she keep this from her knowing Dareyth knows? What significance does he have that gives him the right to know the identity of her father but not her?

Aedlin rolls her shoulders back and tilts her chin up as she approaches Melody who has her sword laid over her lap and a is buffing it lightly with a cloth. She looks up in Aedlin's direction as she gets closer to her.

"Are you ready to go? The preparations at the lake are almost ready, and fae are starting to gather." Melody asks as she gets to her feet and places her sword back in its place on her hip.

"No!" Aedlin shouts, "I'm not ready to go say my final goodbyes to my mother from a script written by someone who knows more about both my mother and me than I do!"

"What are you talking about?" she asks with a raised eyebrow.

"I'm talking about my father! Enough is enough, Melody. Tell me who is. Please."

"You already know." she says quickly and begins to walk away.

"I need to hear you say it." Aedlin mutters.

Melody stops and turns back slowly.

"Aedlin, this is not something you need to concern yourself with. Just go back upstairs, clean your face then meet me back here so we can go to the lake together."

"Damn it Melody I am about to be crowned Queen, I am not a child anymore and you will stop treating me as if I am. I am apparently mature enough to run Malheim." Aedlin shouts and runs a frustrated hand through her hair.

"I am very aware that you are no longer a child, no matter how many spoiled tantrums you throw but given." Aedlin cuts her off.

"Please, just tell me Melody." She once again pleads as tears beginning to fall from her eyes.

"Oh Frayett, please forgive me," Melody whispers before continuing. "Your father is Erevin, the dark elf."

Aedlin's breath hitches in her throat and she chokes

on it. She attempts to pull the front of her chest that is forcing her ribs together.

"Erevin?" She chokes out. "My father is the King of Faulron? As in the place on the side of a cliff where all dark elves live? My father is the most hated man throughout every single city and kingdom across Agoura? My father. . . As in the dark elf who has single-handedly destroyed four separate kingdoms in the last six years and has taken more lives with his own hands than any other King or Queen of Faulron that ever ruled before him?"

Melody looks behind Aedlin then back at her. "It's complicated and now that you know who he is you can understand why your mother wanted this kept from you, now go wash up so we can go."

"I'm not going anywhere. How could you expect me to stand in front of a kingdom of fae who are preparing to look to me as their guide when my father is the reason they are trapped here in the first place?" Aedlin runs her hands through her hair again. "I mean for god's sake, there are fae who lost loved ones because of him.

"Aedlin, I'm warning you; you know enough, now let it go."

Aedlin's vision hazes around the edges and her ears ring. It… It can't be. She looks nothing like an elf, let alone a dark elf. That alone is enough to know that there had obviously been some sort of miscommunication down the line about who her father really is, or maybe her mother lied to everyone to keep the identity of her *real* father a secret. The thought is as ridiculous as it sounds. If Aedlin's mother did lie about the identity of her father, why would she say it was Erevin? But still, there is the burning question that continues to bother her. Why doesn't look like him?

"Why don't I look like him?"

"What?"

"Why don't I look like my father?" Aedlin mumbles, distracted and feeling like her body isn't her own but hoping some straight answers might help.

"You expect me to know why genetics work the way they do and why sometimes children are born looking more like one parent than the other?"

"What I expect from you Melody is for you to tell me the truth."

"We don't have time for this." she says, rushed and a little panicked.

"I'm running this show now, so watch me make the damn time!" Aedlin says through the burning lump in her throat.

Melody's shoulders slump, and she drops her head in defeat. "You *do* look like your father." She begins before taking a pause to calm herself. "There is a fae. She was your mother's best friend since they were children. Besides the Queen's advisor, your mother, her parents and myself, she is the only other who knows the truth about your father's identity. It is because of her that you look nothing like him."

Drums beat loudly somewhere close by; a rhythmic drum beat that matches the ever rapidly growing beating of Aedlin's heart.

Melody's gaze falls to the necklace that sits against Aedlin's chest.

"Come with me. I need to show you something." Melody says suddenly.

She heads back toward the castle, giving Aedlin no chance to argue, so she does as Melody says. Aedlin follows behind as she leads her upstairs and through the corridor that leads to Aedlin's quarters. Melody ignores everyone as they pass, and in return, Aedlin offers each of them an apologetic smile.

She opens the doors to Aedlin's quarters and allows her to enter first. Rather than just closing the door behind her, she locks it, Aedlin raises her eyebrow at her, but Melody ignores it.

"Melody, what are we doing here?"

"Get in the bathroom."

"Why?"

"Just go. I will explain everything if you just listen to me."

The desire to be dismissive creeps in, along with thoughts that Aedlin knows are her better judgement. She's lived her entire life so far, not knowing who her father is. It hasn't affected all that much.. Aedlin's mother was around, but hardly nurturing and barely had the time free to spend with her. She knows she did what she could, but really, the only true parent Aedlin has ever known is Melody. She could continue on the path that had been planned for her since her birth. She could leave this room right now, shove these thoughts and worries somewhere deep inside and attend her mother's funeral. She could read her script and say goodbye to her mother, then begin her place as the Queen of Malheim.

"Maybe we should just go." Aedlin sighs.

"It's too late for that now. You want answers. Here they are." Melody says sharply.

Wearily Aedlin enters the bathroom as Melody had instructed.

"Stand in front of the mirror and face it." She demands.

Confused, but honestly a little curious now, Aedlin once again does as Melody says and stands in front of the mirror. She looks at her reflection for only a moment. The green, wide eyes surrounded by red puffiness and the almost translucent paleness of her skin wasn't what she was expecting to be looking back at her. Aedlin knew she wouldn't look as good as usual, with rosy cheeks and alert eyes, but she certainly didn't expect to almost not recognise herself with the grief and anger today have bought her.

Melody stands behind Aedlin and grabs the clasp of her necklace. As a reflex, Aedlin's hand reaches up to grab the wings that sit against her chest.

"What are you doing?" Aedlin shouts at her.

"Answering your questions, for just a few minutes I need you to let go and trust me."

Aedlin gives the fragile wings one last squeeze, then releases them, balling her hands into fists at her side to fight the urge to stop Melody once again.

Melody unclasps, then removes Aedlin's necklace. She grabs Aedlin's right hand and tells her to open it. She does as she is told, and Melody places the necklace in her open hand.

In just the few seconds that Aedlin's necklace has been anywhere but her neck, she feels completely stripped bare, as if her soul itself is exposed for everyone to see. It's a nakedness that Aedlin has never experienced before and a vulnerableness that makes her want to run and hide somewhere deep and dark. There is a weight missing where the necklace usually sits. It's wrong, almost unbearable. Aedlin separates the clasps with the intention of putting it immediately back on.

Before she can put it back in its place, Melody snatches it out of her hand.

"Look at yourself." Melody whispers.

Without considering why, Aedlin does as Melody says. A bubble of laughter builds up and escapes and Melody's eyes widen in response.

"What sort of sick joke is this?" Aedlin asks through nervous laughter.

"Aedlin, pull yourself together."

"This. Is. Sick." Aedlin manages to say through the laughter that has picked back up.

"Aedlin, that is enough!" Melody grabs Aedlin by the shoulders and holds her in place in front of the mirror.

"Look at yourself." She repeats.

Aedlin's laughter immediately subsides with the urgency of Melody's tone. She glances at her hands before looking back up at the mirror.

"No." She whispers. Oh God's, this just isn't possible.

"My hands… They're … They're turning blue!" Aedlin exclaims, frightened.

This time when Aedlin looks back up at her reflection she can't turn away, her ears have completely changed shape and are now more pointed and larger, her eyes, instead of vibrant green are cloudy and blue, almost the same shade of blue as her face and her usually full, thick hair has thinned out. *This can't be real, this is impossible.* Repeats over and over in her mind as she tries to make sense of what she is seeing.

"That's not me." Aedlin whispers, tears balancing on the edge of the stranger's eyes that look back at her.

"Yes, it is. This is what you *really* look like, without the necklace cloaking your true identity." Melody says, tightening her grip on Aedlin's shoulders. Aedlin has half a mind to shove her away, but she is grateful that it's holding her in place.

she puts her had against her chest where her necklace should be.

"My mother always said it was for my protection. She said that she had one of the Fae bless it with a powerful magic that would always protect me in moments of danger, as long as I never took it off."

"That is *exactly* what she did, and that is exactly what it does. It just doesn't protect you in the way you assumed. It keeps your true identity hidden so you will always have a place among Fae kind without ridicule and shame. "

Aedlin's hands tremble with anger as she looks right at the fae she thought she knew and could trust most in the world.

"The fae-folk of Malheim would have accepted me for who I really am!" Aedlin shouts.

Melody grits her teeth, and her neck muscles tighten. "Perhaps, but your grandparents would not have. They knew who your father was and that brought great shame to them, but your mother suspected correctly that if you looked nothing like your father, they would not force her to abandon you. All she had to do after that was make sure you never found out the truth, so you would one day get to lead the kingdom as a Fae."

Aedlin turns and rips the necklace from Melody's hand and clasps it back in place around her neck. Just as fast as it had changed before her features return.

Turning back to the mirror, Aedlin fixes her hair back into its pins, wipes the tear streaks from her face, and pinches her cheeks a little to get some pink back into her face.

Very quickly Aedlin realises that this is one of those make-or-break decisions life likes to throw. She squares her shoulders and allows herself to accept what she already knows. She has a job to do's the *only* thing that matters right now.

"Come Melody, we're going to be late to my mother's

funeral."

"Aedlin?"

"Now Melody, don't you think I should be setting a good example for our kingdom? What sort of message does it send when the soon to be new Queen shows up late to the funeral of her own mother?"

"Yes, I um, I suppose you're right." Melody stammers, then rushes quickly to Aedlin's side.

"If you need a minute, I can stall them?" Melody offers quietly and a little nervously.

"You will do no such thing!" Aedlin growls before leaving the room."

CHAPTER TWO

The entire kingdom has gathered around the lake by the time Aedlin and Melody arrive. It is almost completely surrounded by Fae, who are waiting silently for the funeral to begin. The sun sits high in the sky directly above them and it takes no time for sweat beads to form on her hairline and brow and for her godforsaken dress to feel like it ways ten tonne more than it did just moments ago. She curses to herself for not thinking to grab the matching handkerchief which had been made at the same time as her dress. She thought it was over the top to have a black handkerchief to wipe her tears with but now she finds herself considering asking Melody to rush back and retrieve it for her. She tries to find a clear path through to where she is expected to stand at the mouth of the lake, she is about to excuse herself as she tries to pass through a young fae with a boyish face, unusually curly hair and a bakers apron but before she could ask him to move she loses her footing and trips, driving the heel of her shoe into the soft dirt.

"Damn." She cusses and straightens herself back out as quickly as she can.

"I am so sorry princes... Ah, I mean Queen... or princess?" the boyish featured fae stumbles as he frantically drops down and attempts to dust off the dirt from the bottom of Aedlin's dress.

Seeing him so worried about a mistake that wasn't even his own makes her feel uncomfortable.

"Please get to your feet and stop fussing. You have nothing to apologise for." Other fae who are standing close by start looking at the both of them and the young fae who is still at her feet notices. He stops touching her dress, but he keeps his eyes low as his cheeks grow as red as rose petals.

Wordlessly Aedlin reaches down and grabs the fae by the hands, he hesitates with his grasp, but Aedlin just hold him tighter and pulls up, getting him to get to his feet. She can feel more fae beginning to stare but she does her best to ignore each of them.

She brushes a lose curl out of the young fae's green eyes and smiles as him. She looks down and notices that he has covered the knees of his pants in dirt.

"I'm sorry your trousers got dirty, if the stains are too tough please have them sent to the castle, I will have one of my staff tend to them." She says sweetly.

"Th…Thank you." He stammers nervously.

She takes pity on the poor boy, she never wants anyone to ever feel as thought they need to be this cautious around her, it would be absolutely exhausting to feel such fear around someone simply because they were born into the family of the Queen.

She places her hand softly under his chin and tilts his head up so he has to look at her.

"Keep your head up, ignore their stares. You did nothing wrong, and you have nothing to fear." She says, trying to reassure him, although, she's not naive enough to think that it will work.

He doesn't say anything, but he gives she a timid smile then steps to the side, allowing her to pass.

Melody places her hand on Aedlin's shoulder as they make their way through the now clear path the fae around them have made.

They get to the open area by the mouth of the lake where Aedlin's mother's body lay on a makeshift raft with a large white cloth laying covered in white lilies over her body, revealing only the silhouette of her underneath. Aedlin finds her place beside Dareyth. He scrunches his nose at her, but she ignores him, keeping her head up and her sight on her mother's body. Aedlin finds herself looking at her mother's chest, waiting to see even the smallest rise, then fall. A heavy shudder ripples through her as she comes to accept the inevitable; she really is gone.

Suddenly Aedlin is very aware that at some point Melody had let go of her shoulder. She turns, panicked, to look for her. Before she can make a full spin, a hand is once again on her shoulder.

"I'm right here." Melody whispers from close behind.

Aedlin places her hand on top of Melody's and gives it a squeeze. She squeezes her shoulder in return and Aedlin's heart swells. It's in that moment she knows what she needs to do. She knows what is expected of her, whether she's ready for it or not. Her mother, Melody and the fae-folk of Malheim need her to step up to the plate and lead them, guide them and keep the peace her mother held for so many years, even if that means answering to those who threaten them. Her priorities must remain in place, just as her mother's always did. Starting with letting go of her today, reading from a carefully crafted script and as of tomorrow taking her place in the throne in front of the entire kingdom.

A group of young fae dressed in traditional warrior clothing approach Aedlin. A young boy walks just a little ahead of the rest of the group with sandy blonde hair and freckles is carrying a huge bunch of lilies. His eyes dart through the crowd as he looks around nervously, but he is careful to keep his head forward. They stop in front of Aedlin and bow their heads. The little boy comes a step closer and hands Aedlin the flowers.

"Thank you so much." She says and ruffles his hair a little. "You were all very brave walking out in front of everyone to gift me these beautiful flowers." She smiles fondly at the lot of them as she watches their smiles spread, she thanks them.

They are ushered away, and music begins to flow through the crowd from somewhere behind them. Its' a soft, song that perfectly sums up the mood of everyone it's engulfing.

The Queens soon –to-be-ex advisor shoves a folded-up piece of paper at Aedlin, it only takes a glance to see that it's the script.

Although she is and will remain completely suspicious of him and has no plans to let him any closer to her then arm's length, ever, she does know that keeping him close means she can keep a better, more watchful eye on him. So, she makes sure to thank him as she takes the paper.

Before opening it to begin speaking Aedlin angles herself slightly back toward Melody.

"I want a warrior fae on Dareyth at all times. I trust you to choose someone you know can be reliable and discreet. Be sure to tell them to keep themselves at a safe distance and report to you the moment they hear or notice something that could endanger or threaten the kingdom in any way." Aedlin whispers.

"Of course. I will see to it immediately after the funeral" she whispers back.

The high priest raises his eyebrow at Aedlin questioningly, but she once again ignores him and instead unfolds the piece of paper and finally begins reading.

"Thank you all so much for being here to show my mother…"

This isn't right at all, just as Aedlin knew it wouldn't be. If she stands any chance of having the Fae of this kingdom trusting her, she needs to show them she actually cares. And if that means tweaking what she's expected to say, just a little, so be it.

Aedlin clears her throat and starts again.

"Thank you all so much for being here to show *our* mother one last time just how much she truly meant to us all. Malheim was always her greatest pride. Every single one of you mattered to her, and she showed that in her dedication to protect us all from those who seek to threaten us…"

A strong jolt pulls at Aedlin's arm, nearly making her trip. Melody has her gripped painfully tight and is trying to pull her toward the crowd.

"We need to go. Right now."

"What?" Aedlin asks, looking around at the confused crowd. Which, at closer inspection, seems to be suddenly missing a large portion of the warrior and healing fae..

"What's going on?" she barely manages to get out as Melody drags her through the remaining fae.

"I will explain as soon as I can. Just follow me."

Aedlin follows her through the crowd of Fae until finally breaking free of them.

"Fly to the castle. I will be right behind you. Just like we've practised." Melody says, gently shoving Aedlin, urging her to go.

Aedlin wants to press her for information, but the warning look Melody is giving her is a look she knows all too well. The only option Melody is about to give her is to do as she's told, so Aedlin does exactly that.

The view of the kingdom from above always has and always will take Aedlin's breath away. Their little hidden away kingdom has everything they could possibly need, from growing their own food, raising their animals to use for extra help around the kingdom and with some of the heavy lifting. One of her favourite places to sneak off to when Melody was otherwise preoccupied was the stables. It takes only a few quick minutes to make it to the courtyard of the castle, then only a few more to race upstairs and into her quarters. Aedlin locks the door behind her. She rushes across the room and grabs the torch that sits above her bed and goes back to stand by the door, waiting to hear from Melody. Five minutes pass… Then ten. She can hardly take it. She wants to look out of one of the windows to see if she can see her coming, but a huge part of this particular drill, Melody practised with her, was for her to stay low and away from the windows.

Aedlin remains crouched by the door, gripping her weapon and keeping her head low while trying to keep away the thought that something bad might have happened to Melody. Her heart drums so loud in her ears she almost can't hear the three knocks against the door. Each one followed by a pause before the next. Aedlin scrambles to her feet then repeats the knocking pattern back and in response there is a single knock that gives Aedlin the confirmation that it's Melody on the other side of the door.

Quickly turning the key and unlocking the door Aedlin starts bombarding her with questions before she manages to open the door properly.

"Melody, tell me what's going on? Is everyone safe?"

Melody pushes past Aedlin and goes to her bedroom, ignoring her questions and pulling Aedlin's cupboard away from the wall.

"Melody please! Just tell me, is the kingdom safe?"

Melody sighs, a long, I don't have time for this kind of sigh before answering. "No, our perimeter has been breached. The alarm was raised right before I escorted you out."

"By who?"

"I don't know yet. I didn't have time to get that information. I need to do my job before joining the others."

Her job? Aedlin thinks angrily. She's wasting her time with her while there is an entire kingdom of Fae who need help below them.

"Melody, your job is not to hold my hand, not anymore. I need you out there, assisting the other warrior Fae and avoiding the intruders reaching Malheim centre and the Elder tree and I should be out there too!"

"And what exactly would you help with? Every other fae in Malheim has been gifted an ability by the elder tree, except you. Everyone who is of age is fully trained in their natural abilities. Those who are not yet of age have enough training to get by. The children were escorted away before you were and were hidden below the chapel. They can hold their own, for now."

"It's my job to help them!" Aedlin pleads with her, not understanding why Melody would let her run and hide when she is needed the most.

"Not yet, it's not!" Melody continues moving the cupboard as Aedlin runs her hands through her hair and looks at Melody in disbelief.

Melody reaches into a hole in the wall Aedlin never knew existed and pulls out what looks like an old, folded up brown blanket.

"Let's go. Stick behind me and stay quiet." Melody demands.

She quickly pushes the cupboard back into place, then, with the brown blanket in hand, leaves Aedlin's bedroom.

Aedlin sticks close to her as best she can, something Melody doesn't make easy as she takes the stairs three at a time. Finally, she stops outside of the door that leads to the dungeons Aedlin's grandparents had built when they established Malheim and had the castle built. Thankfully, as far as Aedlin had always been told anyway, the dungeons were never used. They were always just there as a precaution.

Melody leans in close to the door and whispers something before taking a step back. It sounds as though a heavy sounding lock unhinges from the other side and as soon as it does Melody pulls the door open, grabs Aedlin by the hand, taking her by surprise and pulls her down another flight of stairs. The door closes behind them before they even reach the fifth step.

Torches are positioned sparingly along the damp walls lining the staircase and continue down into the dungeon.

"Am I supposed to hide in here?" Aedlin asks, fed up with the secrecy.

"No." Is all Melody says and continues making her way to the far end of the dungeon, passing all of the metal barred cells until they get to the very last one at the further most end of the room.

Melody stops in front of it and opens the metal door. It lets out a piercing groan that Aedlin is convinced could be heard from upstairs.

Melody steps into the cell and Aedlin's eyes widen with realisation.

"I'm *not* going in there!"

"Aedlin, please. I'm not about to lock you down in the dungeon. Now please, you need to come with me."

She's right, of course Aedlin knows Melody would never do something like lock her down here, even if it was for her own protection. At least, she's pretty sure she wouldn't.

Aedlin continues to follow her but remains cautious. She's not naïve enough to completely let her guard down. Even with someone she's known her entire life who is acting utterly suspicious about everything that's happening outside of the castle right now and, of course, the whole bringing her to the dungeon's situation.

Melody stops in front of the left side of the cell. She once again whispers something, just as she had at the door and once she steps back the dark, wet bricks shift lazily out on themselves until there is a clear doorway revealed.

Melody clicks her fingers and a small ball of light hovers just above her palm. She keeps her fingers slightly raised and not quite touching the ball.

"Come on, we're nearly there." Melody says, rushed and demanding.

Aedlin sticks close behind her in a wordless rush, not wanting to fall behind and risk being stuck in the dark.

She can hardly take the anxiety and uncertainty. Aedlin had always thought she would be happy to blindly follow whatever instructions Melody would give because she had always known Melody took her job far more seriously than any fae Aedlin had ever known. She knew that Melody would protect her until her final breath which is something Aedlin had never hoped it would come to. She doesn't want anyone's life on the line, especially not the Fae who helped raise her. But right now, Aedlin is finding herself having to question everything she thought about Melody and whether she is someone she really can trust as much as she always thought she could.

Before Aedlin gets to attempt once again to get some sort of straight answer from her she stops. The hidden path they had been taking has come to an end and is blocked by a makeshift wall built from large stones. The smell of saltwater travels through the slight cracks carried by a very welcome cool breeze.

"Give me your necklace." she says, reaching out with the hand that is already holding the brown blanket.

"Why?" Aedlin asks, protectively clutching the wings.

"Because I need you to wear this one instead."

She drops the blanket to the ground then leans down

and unfolds it, revealing a necklace in the extremely limited light it appears to be just amethyst connected to a hand-woven rope chain, as well as a small pouch and a small blade with a black and gold hilt that matches Melody's sword exactly.

"Melody! Enough already. You need to tell me what you're doing and why you are making me flee. Deciding I'm just a liability is not a good enough reason. I should be with my people!"

She sighs, picks up the necklace, then gets to her feet.

"I'm not asking you to flee. I'm asking you to locate your mother's old friend, Seiche, and inform her that the kingdom is under attack. She will know exactly what to do. All you must do is get to her cabin just outside the forest that lines the outside of our kingdom, sitting not too far from the shoreline."

Waves of panic shoot all through Aedlin's body.

"But we're never supposed to leave. You're asking me to risk revealing the location of Malheim?"

"No, I'm asking you to save it. Our location and your identity will remain hidden so long as you wear this." she holds up the amethyst necklace for Aedlin to take from her.

"I hardly leave the castle! How do you expect me to navigate through a forest and find someone I've never

44

seen before? There has to be someone here more experienced." Aedlin pleads with her as panic builds. "Maybe you should go? I mean, if this is something that absolutely needs to be done to help Malheim, don't you think it would be for the best if you go yourself to ensure you actually find her?" Aedlin's words come out rushed and panicked and it takes Melody a moment to answer.

"I'm just following orders; it doesn't matter if I think this is a good idea or not. That was never my choice to make."

"Who gave the order?"

"Your mother and after how many promises I made between the two of us I have already broken today, I'm not about to break another."

"It was never fair of her to make you keep my true identity from me." Aedlin says sadly, unable to meet her gaze.

"It was never my place to tell you either way."

Melody looks behind Aedlin and her expression grows more anxious. Melody needs her to do this, and she needs to get back, Aedlin knows it must be driving Melody crazy being a warrior fae with natural instincts as strong as hers and not be out with the rest of her guild where she knows she should be, protecting Malheim.

"Okay," Aedlin finally says. "What else do I need to

do?"

CHAPTER THREE

Aedlin stands looking down the cliff to the beach below, where gentle waves rock a small sail boat, she chuckles to herself in disbelief knowing full well that this cannot be the boat Melody was talking about. A wind, stronger than she has ever felt before within the confines of the kingdom, whips her hair around and fills her lungs with salty air. The boat below is the only one in view, but how did Melody expect her to get to it if she's not able to use her wings?

She takes a quick look behind herself. There is no one around, though, She knew that already. Melody had made sure of it after breaking down the wall of stone that divided those in the castle with the world outside. with the hilt of her sword. Surprisingly, it only took five good hits and there was a gap big enough for the both of them to climb through.

She pulls the sides of the brown cloak that she thought had been a blanket tighter around her front to shield herself from the harsh, icy winds coming off the ocean. She had seen paintings of it, of course. She's certain there is even a painting in the castle of this exact location, but it doesn't compare at all. The painting could never capture the smell of salt, the sound of the seagulls flying not too far out from the cliff-side, or the sound of the waves crashing against the shore.

She takes in a breath that feels more cleansing than any she has ever taken before. The wind whips her hair around her face as more and more of it loosens from the elastic that had been holding it in place. She tucks as much as she can back behind her ear and pauses for a moment as she stares at her hand. To her surprise there isn't much, if anything, different about her hands and arms, but she knows there will be dramatic differences in her face and likely ears.

In a single moment of what feels like selfishness given the importance of what she is supposed to be doing; she wishes one of the items Melody had given her had been a mirror. It's not every day you see yourself as an elf when you've lived your whole life as a Fae, then again, she had already seen what she looks like when she allows the dark elf within her to be seen, perhaps looking at herself as someone she doesn't recognise is something she only needs to do once today. Right now, her priorities need to be figuring out how to get down to the boat and, more important than that, hope that it doesn't take all that long to figure out how to use the thing. Melody went over some basics, but Aedlin worries that hearing what to do and actually putting it into effect are two very different things.

Walking closer to the edge of the cliff, Aedlin peers over again to look for another way down. Melody stressed how absolutely important it was for her to never remove the necklace and reveal her true identity as a Fae until she gets to Seiche and although it is very clear that no one else is here, or anywhere near here the idea of already going against what Melody asked makes Aedlin's stomach knot with guilt.

She wants desperately to turn back, find Melody and tell her she needs to handle this herself like they both know she should have from the start, but that option went out the window within minutes of Melody climbing back through to the tunnel. The shield that blocks them from the rest of Agoura is in full effect, even from where they had exited now and all she sees is a thick, uninviting forest with groans from unfamiliar beasts and smells that make the non-existent contents of her stomach want to come back up. Just as Aedlin and anyone else is supposed to see and experience who dares approach the *forbidden forest illusion* her grandparents had created to help keep the location of Malheim a secret. It's clear albeit terrifying; the only choice she has is to get down the cliff and on the sailboat.

Reluctantly she kicks her high heeled boots off and with nerves that make her shake enough to potentially throw off her balance she finds the best place on the cliff to begin her descent down to the sailboat. She tosses her boots down the cliff and watches them fall to the beach below with a now even tighter stomach full of nerves.

"Okay, stop stalling". She mumbles to herself. She turns, facing her back to the ocean, finding her footing and going by feel she begins making her way down the cliff, making sure to keep track of her footing so she can grab hold of those same areas with her hands after stepping down further to avoid the risk of slipping as much as possible.

Both her feet and the tips of her fingers burn relentlessly before she's even halfway down making it harder to keep her footing and get a good grip. The cold air coming in from the ocean gets stronger and the feel of it forcing her against the hard rock that makes up the side of the of the cliff makes her lose focus. She missteps and begins to slip. Frantically Aedlin claws at the mountain, crying out in pain as the skin on her fingers gets torn to shreds, staining the mountain red with her blood. A gurgled scream comes out. It sounds completely foreign and if she wasn't descending to her inevitable death she would probably be inclined to look around and make sure someone else isn't in some sort of danger nearby. Perhaps there is someone else on the shore of the beach. At least that would mean there is no reason for her body to have to just lay and rot. Well, not *her* body, not really. What if Melody thinks she was a coward and ran from the responsibility she now has as Malheim's Queen? No one is going to recognise her so no one will know to take her home or to even try to find more fae-kind, which is of course, the point of being hidden. she guesses that's the one thing that no one considered when hiding them away from everyone else. Eventually someone was going to have to leave and the only way they would be able to return is if they were still alive. But as grim as it is she knows in her heart she would have made the same decision. Forever losing someone when who has died whilst outside of the protective walls that shielded them all from the outside seems like such a small price to pay for keeping the lives of everyone else and the elder tree safe.

"Let yourself fall; I'll catch you."

Aedlin ignores the impossible voice that had to be her mind playing tricks on her and continues to try to grab at the seemingly never ending cliffside.

"You need to let yourself fall back. It will make it easier for me to catch you."

In response to the stranger's words, Aedlin quite literally takes a leap of faith. Surprising herself enough to let out another fear-filled Yelp. The wind rushes past her and her heart drums violently. With one final sharp breath she prepares for impact and hopes with everything she has that she survives the landing. She has had one job so far as the almost Queen of Malheim. As much as she has come to accept her inevitable demise in the last twenty seconds it absolutely does not mean she doesn't hope to walk away from this and carry out what Melody has asked of her.

She hits something with a thud and prepares for the pain. It doesn't come until after she's fallen back. Her ribs cry out, her back does the same and she suspects she's done something to her left foot yet, surprisingly her head feels somewhat- okay besides a little pressure.

She lays still, wanting to just test parts of her body but at a time to assess the damage.

"Do you mind if we get up now?" someone groans

right beside her ear.

Aedlin jumps up in surprise and lets out a gasp. Defensively, she reaches for the knife Melody gave her and takes a few cautious steps back, keeping her eyes on the elf that lay on the ground. Her hands tremble. It could be adrenaline from the fall, but more likely it's the fear that's tightening her stomach.

"Who are you?"

He gives no answer but climes to his feet and wipes away the blood that is running from his nose. It's pointless. The blood continues to run steadily, ruining his black tunic.

"I'm Saviel. And you are welcome." He bears a toothy grin and winks at Aedlin. Completely ignorant of how ridiculous he looks behaving like that, while blood freely falls from his face.

"Th... Thank you." Aedlin stammers, giving him a polite nod before shakily making her way toward the boat that sits alone along the small pier just a little in the distance along.

"Are you sure you should be walking? Maybe you should get checked over by someone?" he says, following close behind.

Aedlin instinctively places her hand back on the handle of her knife that sits hidden within the shallow pocket of her dress.

"Thank you for your concern, but I'm sure I will be fine." She slows her steps to better hear how close he is walking behind her.

"Can I at least ask what it is that's so important you would risk your life trying to make your way down that cliff?"

"No. you may not ask."

The distance between her and the small, more beat up than she could tell from the top of the cliff sailboat closes.

Saviel falls into step beside her, and she pulls the knife out just enough to ensure she can react in time if he tries anything, but still not enough for him to see it.

She keeps her eyes on the boat ahead of her, uncomfortably aware that he is staring at her.

"I've never seen you around here before."

"Is that supposed to be a question?"

"No, just an observation I guess." Saviel says with a shrug.

"Perhaps you could keep your observations to yourself and stop following me?"

"I just saved your life. What kind of thank you is

walking away and making it very clear you're not interested in holding a conversation with me?"

"I already thanked you. If you'd like, I'm happy to do it again - if it means you will take a hint and see that I have somewhere I need to be, alone."

Aedlin hates that she is being so rude to a complete stranger, especially a complete stranger who—as he said just saved her life, but she can't risk anyone knowing who she really is, what she's doing or learning the location of Malheim.

"You're not very trusting, are you?" Saviel asks, his mouth spreading into a sarcastic smile.

"You're overly trusting, aren't you?" Aedlin reiterates.

"Not particularly, but I do find I'm quite caring, so when I notice a damsel in distress falling from the side of a cliff, I don't see that I have any choice but to offer my assistance, including lingering with you for a while to ensure you have your wits about you, especially if you plan on trying to row yourself anywhere in that." He points to the boat they are now standing right in front of and scrunches his face up at the sight of it.

With a deep exhale, Aedlin turns to face Saviel. She needs to get on that boat and locate Seiche; she doesn't have the time to pass pleasantries with Saviel.

"Look, I can barely begin to express how grateful I am to you for saving my life, it wasn't just my life you saved, and that is something I could never repay you for, perhaps someday we could meet again, and I will have the time to hold a decent conversation with you but now is not that time,"

The blood on Saviel's nose has dried, which will make it harder for him to clean easily. Without a second thought, Aedlin removes her blade from her dress pocket and uses it to cut a small section of her now filthy cloak.

"Stay here for a moment." Aedlin says, ignoring his puzzled look. She dips the torn off cloak in the crystal-clear waters on the shore of the beach until the water running off the material is clear, wring it out then carry it the five steps back to him and pass it to him.

"For your nose." she says quietly.

He takes it from her and says, "Thank you." With an embarrassed smile he immediately wipes the blood from his nose.

"Don't mention it." Aedlin shrugs before turning away back toward the boat.

"Stop!" Saviel calls out after her.

She rolls her eyes in frustration but stops and turns back to face him.

"Yes?"

"I can't, in good conscious let you get in that boat. I have one not too much further down the shore. Let me take you wherever it is you're trying to get."

"I don't know…" Aedlin says, as she considers the likelihood of staying with Saviel for too long, making it more likely for something to go wrong.

"Don' t think of it as doing a favour for you, if that's what your problem is. You would actually be helping me out a lot because if I have to spend the rest of my life wondering if that boat sank while you were trying to sail it, I imagine it would put a pretty grey cloud over my life."

Aedlin looks around nervously. Of course, she knows it would make trying to find Seiche's house a lot easier if she travelled with someone who actually knew how to sail. Especially if that someone had any idea of the location she was looking for. But still, although she lived a quite sheltered life, Aedlin knows better than to get in a damn boat with a stranger.

"Look, I really don't think this is a good idea, but I would prefer to not end up stranded in the damn ocean because I don't know how to sail and even if I did, it's a miracle that boat is afloat as it is." She says as she slips her boots back on.

Aedlin makes sure to take a mental note – the very first thing she will be doing on her return to Malheim, after making sure the kingdom is safe is to chew her out for sending her on this impossible task in the first place, let alone expecting me to be able to actually carry out her request on a sailboat with no idea how to sail, especially on a boat that looks old enough to have been left here sometime before my grandparents moved here.

Aedlin sighs, a sigh full of frustration and fear, but also relief and gratefulness for the mysterious elf who by some miracle has in just a few minutes managed to save her life and will be able to get her to the fae who will save her kingdom.

Saviel finishes wiping his face and scrunches the torn off, now blood-stained piece of cloak in his hand.

"Alright then, just tell me where it is you need to go and the Ellenier will get you there." Saviel says with a smile that Aedlin suspects is full of pride.

"I'm sorry, Ellenier?" Aedlin asks, confused. If there is someone else here, why hasn't she noticed them yet? Or why would Saviel wait until now to mention them? Perhaps they have been waiting on the boat for Saviel to return.

"That's the name of my boat." he says with a shrug and walks past Aedlin in the opposite direction to the boat shaped pile of wood and yellow stained material that makes up the sail.

"You coming?" Saviel asks from a distance further than Aedlin had been expecting.

"Yeah, sorry." Aedlin says and jogs to catch up to Saviel.

They round a corner not too far up from where Aedlin fell to what should have been her death. The beach narrows off almost completely and right at the very edge of the sand sits another sailboat. It's bigger, but not too much bigger than the one she was supposed to use and in far better condition. The side of the boat, at what Aedlin is pretty sure is called the stern is the name Ellenier hand painted in blue.

Aedlin stops just a few feet away from the boat, her eyes wide and her chest compressing painfully in itself.

"Is everything okay?" Saviel calls out from the boat.

Aedlin isn't sure what to say. Truthfully, she isn't completely sure what is causing her hesitation. All she knows is something deep in her core wants nothing to do with getting on that boat with a stranger. But what choice does she have? Her kingdom is relying on her to save them, and she has already wasted far too much time as it is. With a shuddered breath, Aedlin shoves her negative, intuitive thoughts deep into some place easier to ignore and climbs the small ramp leading up to the side of the boat. As soon as Aedlin is on the boat and after Saviel gives her a polite, awkward smile that she somehow translated to 'you're in the way' she moves to the side and Saviel drags the plank onto the boat and slides it under a wooden seat that runs just short enough across the boat to leave room on either side for someone to walk.

"So, where to, junior sailor?" Saviel asks. Aedlin takes a seat and watches with genuine interest as he starts untying and tying off knots.

"There is a house on the other side of the forbidden forest. It sits between the edge of the forest, and she shore of the ocean. I know it's not much to go on. I'm sorry, but that description is all I have."

"No need to apologise, luckily for you. I know the place."

Aedlin doesn't even try to hide the surprise from her face. If he knows the house, she is talking about that could mean he knows Seiche and if he knows her; he knows she is a Fae. She studies his expression; he seems relaxed, maybe even happy. He has a confident swagger about him as he makes his way around his boat, effortlessly like sailing. It is as natural as breathing to him.

The boat pulls away from the shoreline and out toward the open ocean. If he does know Seiche he doesn't appear to have any negative thoughts about what she is.

She continues to watch him, feeling completely un-helpful but also too scared to ask if he needs any help in case he actually says yes. She knows he would be lying about needing it, of course. But something about him tells her that he is the type to say he wants help just so he can get the chance to show off his skills at a closer range. He's hands are a little calloused. She had noticed it ear-lier and figured he must work with his hands a lot, but watching him know she wouldn't be surprised if he got them from sailing alone.

He's square jaw relaxes and tightens depending on whether the task he is completing wants to cooperate eas-ily or not. The muscles in his arms flex as he pulls on one of the ropes. Aedlin takes notice that his black tunic and pants are a little tight fitting on him and worn in the knees.

Saviel finishes up with the rope and takes a seat beside Aedlin. Some of his dark hair has fallen forward over his face and he brushes it out of the way, running his hands through it. Aedlin gasps a loud gasp, followed by a hard gulp and warm, pink cheeks.

"Is everything okay?" Saviel asks, his brow lowers with concern.

"Yeah." Aedlin says unintentionally sharply, but being embarrassed tends to give her a bit of a snappy attitude problem. It always has.

Saviel seems to shrug it off and Aedlin relaxes in response. She leans back a little, allowing herself for just a few moments to feel the warmth of the sun on her skin, to let the smell and sounds of the ocean surrounding them fill her very soul and for what feels like the first time in her life she allows herself to breathe.

Her moment of peace is short-lived. Just as soon as she had allowed herself to feel it, the black cloud filled with her new found responsibility rolls back in. She never assumed for a second having to watch over, protect and maintain Malheim would have ever been easy, but never having to leave the safety of the protective shell that holds everyone she loves in its place feels, compared to being out here and having feels like it would have been far less complicated.

"So?" Saviel says, leaning forward and resting his arms on his knees. "Am I allowed to know why you risked your life to get to this house?"

Aedlin looks out toward the forest they are passing. The tree line ends not too far up from where they are now, and she breathes a sigh of relief that they are making faster time than she had anticipated.

"I just need to check on her, it's important that I make

sure she hasn't fallen ill." Aedlin watches Saviel's reaction closely, holding her breath until he gives her an understanding smile.

"Well, good thing we are almost there. That definitely sounds important enough to almost lose your life over."

"Thank you for doing this for me." Aedlin says, dropping her gaze as she does. Perhaps eventually she will be able to handle moments like this, moments where she lets through her vulnerability to anyone who isn't her mother or Melody.

"Don't mention it, like I said, you're really doing me a favour."

"If you would prefer to see it that way, let's go with it." Aedlin says with a small, bubble of a laugh.

CHAPTER FOUR

"Please could you wait outside? Honestly you would be helping me out so much if you could just keep watch for me. I know you have already done so much, and I swear I will find some way to repay you. Just please, do this one last thing for me."

Aedlin had considered just parting way with Saviel as soon as they reached the shore. She was going to thank him, wish him well and go their separate ways. But she hadn't anticipated seeing people so close to both the house and the tree line of the forbidden forest. She needs to be sure no one is going to come in while she is there and the best way to do that is ask Saviel for his help.

Saviel looks around nervously. The uncertainty is obvious in his eyes, but Aedlin can't allow him to come inside like he had requested when they were getting off the boat without exposing herself and the kingdom to him. He might be nice enough to get on a boat with, he was even nice enough to save my life, but neither of which is enough to trust that I can tell him who I really am without repercussion.

"keep watch for what exactly?" he asks, defeated.

"Please, just don't let anyone in while I'm inside."

"I need you to know that I think it would be a better idea if I was in there with you, but fine. I will keep watch, but if something even looks like it's going south, I'm coming in. There is a settlement of barbaric halflings not too far from here. They often come out as far as the beach, so there is a very real chance of running into them."

Aedlin fights the urge to hug her arms around herself protectively. "I will be in and out as fast as I can. Thank you so much for doing this for me. I promise, as soon as I am done inside, you are free to be rid of me."

Saviel chuckles a little, but his smile is conflicted. Aedlin chooses to pretend she didn't notice. It's not something she has time to dwell on right now.

Aedlin leaves Saviel standing a few feet from the house and approaches the door of the wooden cottage that is surrounded by a beautiful and well-kept flower garden. She knocks three times, one after the other, with shaky hands.

The door opens only seconds later and Aedlin's eyes widen as they fall on the woman in front of her, the very human woman with greying hair that doesn't quite match the age of her soft featured face. Her blue eyes are pale around the edges and are wide as she looks at Aedlin.

"Is there something I can help you with, miss?" Seiche asks, her words slow and full of careful suspicion. She dusts her hands over the apron that drapes around her waist over the top of her green gown.

"This is a conversation that should be had inside, without the risk of prying ears." Aedlin says, keeping her tone hushed but loud enough for Seiche to hear.

"With all due respect, I am not letting you in my home just because you tell me you should."

Aedlin looks around nervously, trying to work out how to tell her who she is without having to use those exact words, just in case she isn't who she is supposed to be. But then she realises she doesn't have to say a thing. Instead, she pulls undies on her cloak and pulls the necklace Melody gave her out from under her dress. Seiche immediately grabs Aedlin's arm and pulls her inside, shutting the door quickly behind them.

Seiche pulls Aedlin into a tight bear hug, taking her by surprise and making her gasp. After Aedlin is pretty sure she has no air left in her lungs Seiche finally let's go and steps back from her.

"Oh, my darling child. I had hoped to never have to see you, at least not like this. Come, we don't have much time."

Seiche rushes toward the back of the cottage, passing through the small living room with an open fire that's burning, which seems odd given the gorgeous weather outside.

"Through here." Seiche says opening a door off the kitchen.

The room is small and stuffy and lit only by a handful of candles places around the room. There are no windows and the door they enter through is the only one in the room. A small table with a large book sits in the middle of the room.

The book's pages are stained and worn, and the binding is falling apart.

Aedlin wants to ask about it, but she doesn't get the chance before Seiche flips through the pages of the book so fast Aedlin almost gets dizzy watching her. She finally stops on a page and immediately begins reading aloud it. Words that sound similar to the ones Melody had said earlier to open the door. Words that come forward from the very back of her memory. She couldn't translate them if she tried, but she does recognise something about them.

There is an enormous crash somewhere outside of the room. Like doors and windows have been blown open. The ocean outside was suddenly alive and angry with the sound of waves slamming their way to the shore.

Seiche continues reading from the page and the wind outside continues to grow. It whistles through the walls of the house, making things fall to the ground all throughout the cottage.

Then just as soon as it had started, everything stops and an eery silence falls over them.

Seiche immediately begins rushing around the room, shoving things into a bag that she pulls out of a cupboard. She starts with the book, then pulls out items from drawers and cupboards around the room.

She blows out the candles one by one and rushes past a stunned and confused Aedlin. Leaving her standing in the room alone.

"Ah… Seiche?" she calls out, leaving the room to follow her and feeling beyond anxious.

"Don't worry, I've taken care of it. Malheim is safe. I have hidden them in plain sight, sort of like what your necklace does. Speaking of. You cannot return home, not for at least a few days, perhaps a week, perhaps more."

Seiche continues rushing around, this time grabbing bread and some fruit from the kitchen to add to her bag.

"I can't go home?"

"No, you need to give it some time. The spell I used is hiding them, but because you are outside of the kingdom, it doesn't affect you. While you're out here, lie low, keep to yourself and for the love of everything. Do not let yourself be known to any of the dark elf king's men- so basically, don't let yourself be known to anyone.'"

"Spell? Wait, no, hold on, just a minute. I have absolutely no knowledge of any spells, yet I know I recognised at least some of what you read from that book."

"You know it because I taught your mother a nursery rhyme that has been passed down through my family for years. She used to sing it to you all the time when you were young. Only ever in secret, of course. My direct blood line is the only fae permitted knowing our ancient language anymore. It's been that way since long before your grandparents came along. That nursery rhyme and the spell have a lot of the same words. I would happily translate for you, but I have no time."

"That can't be true, Melody used magic, just this morning."

"To open the door that leads to the dungeons and again once you were in the cell. Yes, I'm aware, she did exactly as your mother, and I had instructed her to do. I taught her what she needed to know."

Before Aedlin can push further Saviel busts through the door.

"We need to go, right now."

"Take her to Khard." Seiche demands.

By the time Aedlin turns back around to ask Seiche what is going on she is already gone.

"Now Aedlin!" Saviel shouts.

She follows him out the door and goes to turn back toward the beach where they left the boat.

"No, we can't use it now. It's too late." He grabs Aedlin by the arm, ignoring her awkward footing while she tries to keep up.

"Where are we going?" she yells at him.

"I'm getting you to Khard. We will lose them in Mal-kard forest, but not if we don't move it."

"Is it the halflings?" she asks, already having a hard time catching her breath.

"No, a human, he was watching me for a while from near the entrance to the forbidden forest, as soon as that woman you were seeing used that spell he got on his horse and left in a hurry, and I know exactly where he is going."

"You know she used magic?"

"Of course, I know she used magic, as did everyone else who was anywhere near us when she used it. When using it is something you can be punished for by death, you tend to make sure you know what it looks like when it's being used so you can get the hell away from who-ever it is who used it."

Saviel pulls on Aedlin's arm harder as he runs faster. She fights through the developing pain in her feet and continues to match Saviel's speed.

By the time they break the tree line, Aedlin's feet are blistered, her calves ache, sweat soaks through her dress to her cloak and every breath is a sharp burst. She allows them to continue into the forest for a few minutes, far enough that when she looks back, she can no longer make out the break in the trees where they entered from. As soon as it's gone from view, she plants her heels and yanks her arms from Saviel's grip.

"We have to keep going." He pleads, this time at-tempting to grab her hand. Aedlin slaps his hand away and steps back from him.

"And I need to breathe. For heaven's sake, I'm in a cloak and a corset back dress! If we don't stop for a damn minute to let me catch my breath, I'm going to drop dead running for my life."

Saviel runs his hands through his hair and sighs, exasperated.

"One minute, that's it, then we need to continue on. We just need to make sure we get deep enough into the forest. We should have bought ourselves some time, but not enough yet. We are on foot; they will be travelling by horseback so the time I'm trying to buy us is limited."

Aedlin contemplates removing her shoes but decides against it, knowing that blisters are going to be a lot nicer than all of the cuts, scrapes, prickles and stabs her bare feet will endure on the forest floor.

She unties her cloak and lets it fall to the ground around her feet then bends over, resting her hands on her knees and focuses on catching her breath. Remaining hunched over she looks up through her lashes to see Saviel watching her, his shoulders rise and fall faster than they would if they hadn't just been running for their lives, but still, besides that and the beads of sweat formed on his brow and hairline you wouldn't suspect anything was happening. Meanwhile, Aedlin is about at the point where she is wheezing, and she is dripping sweat from all kinds of unmentionable places. She knows it's ridiculous, but it makes her hate him, it's absurd, its immature, but damn it why should he get to stand there like everything is fine?

Aedlin picks her cloak back up from the ground and ties it back into place.

"We should keep moving, like you said." Aedlin walks past him, hoping to get a head start, she knows it won't last, not with her having to run in this damned dress, let alone the cloak and shoes, but still, she makes it a point to at least try to keep up with him without having to be physically pulled along by him.

* * * *

Aedlin can't tell how much time has passed when Saviel finally decides they can rest again. She just knows that now that she can stop, she gets to muster the last of her strength to punch him right in his face. She needs to channel all the pain that is ripping through her muscles into something, and her mind is telling her releasing it into his face feels like the perfect relief and she almost did it, she would have if it wasn't for the sound of a stream nearby. So instead of punching him, she races toward it, ignoring him calling after her and asking where she is going, ignoring the screaming pain and the stench of her sweat.

The sound of the stream grows louder as she approaches. She can almost taste it. She would salivate for it if her mouth wasn't as dry as stone.

Finally, it comes into view and immediately Aedlin removes her cloak and boots.

"Would you mind giving me a hand?" Aedlin asks, not able to meet Saviel's eyes.

"With what?"

"I can't get myself out of this dress. Corset back." She shrugs.

"We really don't have the time."

"Please, do you have any clue how it feels to have to run in something as heavy as this? I need to breathe." She pleads.

He sighs but stands behind her and begins to unfasten the ribbon holding the back of her dress together. The warmth of his breath tickles the back of her neck and it send a shiver through her body and makes the depths of her stomach clench and flutter.

He finishes loosening her dress and steps back, allowing her space. She turns to thank him, but he already has his back turned to her.

She lets he dress fall to her feet, leaving just her slip dress and underwear. She wraps her knife in it, then removes her shoes and walks into the water. She finds her balance on the slippery stones below her feet and watches as the water washes away the blood from her feet.

Saviel rushes in from somewhere behind her. She turns back to see him, eyes wide and panicked, and this time his breathing matches hers.

"What in the world are you doing?"

Aedlin makes a point to lower down and scoop up some water in her hands, then tips her cupped hands back, gulping the water down. She means to answer Saviel, but instead she repeats the process of scooping the water and gulping it down. She doesn't stop until she starts hiccupping and her stomach hurts.

She hiccups again, and Saviel snickers from behind her.

She turns and realises that he has come closer to her. Aedlin takes advantage of the situation and leans down, making it look like she is going to scoop up more water to drink.

"Maybe you should slow down? Those are some pretty serious sounding hiccups."

A smile spreads across Aedlin's face. Saviel notices

it just a second too late and doesn't jump back in time before Aedlin splashes the water she had scooped up at him, wetting his pants below the knees.

She suppresses her laugh, watching with amusement as he shakes his head disapprovingly and doing a terrible job at trying not to smile.

"Don't you need a drink?" Aedlin asks, now frowning and a little concerned about his health.

"Sure, but I think I would prefer to be smart and collect some to take with us."

"Well, that would be wonderful, but to do that, we would need something to collect it in." Aedlin says smugly.

Saviel wordlessly unhooks the empty flask from the back of his pants that had been behind his cloak. He leans down to the water and lets it flow in until the flask is full. He takes a large drink of it for himself, then tops it up again.

"We shouldn't stay here much longer. If the king's men are still looking for us, they will probably stop here, assuming we have done exactly what we have, and stopped for a drink and rest."

Aedlin nods. She is definitely not ready to have to move on from the relief of the cool water, but she gets out anyway and picks up her belongings from the ground.

"Why is it such a problem to use magic? There should be magic using folk all around. Healers, planters…"

Saviel cuts her off and his face pales.

"How could you not know?"

"It's a long story, maybe one for another time."

Saviel looks at Aedlin wearily, but to her surprise, he lets it go.

"Magic has been banned for years now. At first it was just in some places, but now it's across the entirety of Agoura. Anyone caught using magic is sentenced to death, or worse, if the dark elf King finds you useful, he will keep you to use you. I'm not sure if I believe that, though. No one has ever witnessed anyone who had been caught by the king's guard being used."

Aedlin's mouth falls open at his words.

"Is there no one who has tried to stand against him?" Aedlin asks, pulling her cloak tighter around herself, feeling a chill that she's not sure is from the late afternoon wind or the knowledge that her father is exactly who she had been told he is. A monster, a huge part of what makes her who she is, is a ruthless murderer. She never even liked the spiders in her room being killed. Only ever removed and placed in the garden. How is it possible that she could be directly connected to the most feared man in all of Agoura?

"Of course, there have been men, great men who have stood against King Erevin. Men who stood tall and proud, even in the moments the King ripped their final breaths from their chests. But one man against an army of many will never hold strong." Saviel frowns and shakes his head slowly. He kicks the dirt below his leather boots up and lets out a heavy sigh. He opens his mouth like he wants to say something but closes it again, deciding against it. Aedlin decides not to push it. The darkening of his eyes and the deepening of his frown are enough for her to know that whatever is on his mind is something he is struggling with.

"We should keep moving. We only have a few hours left until sunset and once it comes, we'll make camp for the night."

Aedlin reluctantly gets out of the water. She's annoyed by the idea of having to put her dry dress back over her wet slip and body.

"Get behind me!" Saviel growls, and he grabs Aedlin's arm and pushes her behind him.

"What are you doing?" she demands.

"Someone is coming. Just stay quiet. I should be able to move them along."

Aedlin wants to protest but decides against it when two dark elves come into view from the same path they had been on before stopping at the water. She colour of their skin, shape of their ears and blue of their eyes all make her stomach churn. She's one of them, and she's not sure that is something she can ever accept. She does her best to keep her face expressionless.

"You two need any help with directions?" one of them asks in a forced, friendly tone.

"No thank you, we are just here for a swim, then we will be on our way back home."

"And where *exactly* is home?"

"Right here in Malkard." Saviel says sharply.

Aedlin's sight locks onto her dress right at her feet where her knife is buried within its folds.

"Um, you gentlemen wouldn't mind if I get dressed, would you?" she asks with a shy smile and her arms crossed over her chest.

"I don't know. I think I'd mind a little." One of them purrs, making the other chuckle.

"Let's try to have some manners in front of the lady." Saviel says dryly and reaches behind him to rest his hand on Aedlin's arm.

"Let her get dressed."

"Stupid boy, do you not know who we are?"

"Of course I do. You are both on patrol for King Erevin. But I don't care you are or how fearful I am supposed to be of him or you, you will allow her to put her clothes on."

One of the dark elves steps closer to Saviel and his hand tightens on Aedlin.

"You see, now I look live we've got ourselves a problem, because unluckily for you, I don't take too well to being told what to do."

"Funny that, coming from one of King Erevin's cowardly rats." Saviel spits.

The dark elf's face contorts into a snarl, and he lunges forward toward Saviel. Saviel tries to shove Aedlin out of the way so he can jump back, but she is already on the ground. She retrieves her blade, gets to her feet, and shoves Saviel to the side just in time for the dark elf to lunge at her. She drives her blade deep into his stomach, stopping him in his tracks and making him gasp. She pulls the blade back out, and he drops to his knees in front of her. The other guard realises what has happened as Aedlin stands frozen in place, staring at the blood covered blade in her hand.

The other guard sprints toward Aedlin but her feet refuse to move. She can barely make out the faint sound of

Saviel shouting her name somewhere in the distance.

She continues to stare at her juddering hand as some sort of commotion ensues around her.

Just as soon as the chaos started, it's over again and Saviel is beside her and wrapping his hand around hers, trying to shake her blade loose but she can't seem to let go.

"Aedlin, it's over, you're safe now. But we won't be for long if we don't move now." His voice becomes clearer, and her hand releases the blade. It drops to the ground at her feet.

"Get dressed." Saviel demands as he picks her blade up and rushes over to the water to wash it off.

She gets back into her dress and boots. Saviel hands her blade back to her and she slips it back into her pocket as Saviel rushes to do her dress back up for her before putting her robe back on for her.

"I need to know you're ready to run."

"I'm... I'm ready. Aedlin stammers.

He nods, then grabs her hand and leads her back into the forest, continuing the same way they had already been travelling.

* * * *

Nightfall comes faster than either of them had anticipated. The little light left far above them in the sky struggles to break through the canopy of leaves above them. Saviel continues to lead the way for as long as possible, but after the third time Aedlin trips over herself, Saviel decides it's no use trying to go any further tonight.

"I will get a fire lit." Saviel says quietly.

Aedlin doesn't say anything, just removes her cloak and lays it out on the ground by her feet, close to where Saviel is beginning to form sparks on a small pile of dry leaves.

"Is there anything I can help you with?" Aedlin asks, but secretly hoping he says no. She has only just sat down, and her legs are burning fiercely. She's not sure if she could get up if she wanted to.

"No, I've got this." Saviel says with the flash of a genuine grin before leaning down and blowing onto the small flame. It grows larger and he quickly tosses a few surrounding twigs on and gives it another blow.

"I'm going to find some decent logs. I won't be going too far. Just stay here and try to keep the fire burning for me until I get back." He gets up from the ground and immediately heads to the left. Aedlin loses sight of him quickly but focuses on the sound of his footsteps.

"Sure, no problem." She whispers shakily into the darkness behind Saviel.

She hugs her arms around herself protectively. She keeps her eyes on the flickering fire in front of her and continues to focus on Saviel's quietening footsteps. She strains so hard to keep hold of Saviel's footsteps so hard that her ears begin to ring.

"Saviel?" she whispers into the night, but there is no response, and she has lost the sound of him, replaced instead by the ever-growing thud in her chest, getting louder and faster with every beat.

She hears a twig snap from somewhere behind her. She lets out a yelp and gets to her feet, grabbing her knife out as she does in one swift move.

She turns and with a shaky hand holds out her blade toward the darkness. Every breath she exhales condenses in front of her in the cold air.

Whoever it is gets closer, quickly. Their footsteps are sluggish. Perhaps that is how Aedlin can get the advantage over them. She will struggle to see them, but she knows she can be quick on her feet when she needs to be. Melody made sure of that.

She adjusts her stance, placing one foot slightly in front of the other, ready to leap at whoever breaks through the tree line in front of her.

"Aedlin? Is everything okay?" Saviel asks as he approaches her. He drops the pile of logs he is holding and runs to her.

Aedlin continues to tremble. She knows that the sounds must have been coming from Saviel, but she can't seem to put her knife away.

"Aedlin!" Saviel whispers urgently, leaning in close enough for his breath to tickle the side of her face.

"I… Ah… yeah, everything is okay." She puts the knife back in its place.

"Are you sure?"

"Yeah, I'm sure. I just wasn't expecting you to end up behind me."

"Sorry, I didn't mean to startle you." He steps back and in the dying light of the now dying flame, Aedlin can just make out the shape of Saviel's smile.

Aedlin's cheeks pink at the sight and though she knows he can't see her well enough to see her in this state, she still turns back to the fire and sits back down on her cloak.

Saviel picks up one of the logs and brings it over to the fire. He places another handful of nearby dry leaves and twigs on the glowing light and once again lights a match, re igniting it.

He waits for the flames to pick up a bit before adding the log. Once he is done, he removes his cloak and places it on the ground, just as Aedlin had, and sits on it. They remain in a silence for long enough that the fire grows big enough to block their view of each other.

"What were you doing on that cliff? The only way to get up there would be to go through the forbidden forest, which isn't possible, well, so I've heard."

Aedlin's heart rate picks up as panic sets in. She hadn't planned on having to come up with a cover story for anyone. She thought she would have been home by now, so why would she need to worry about it? Her mind races with explanations, anything but the truth. No matter how helpful Saviel has been, she can't let him in. She can't expose Malheim like that.

"I'm don't know." She lies. "I woke up on top of the cliff. I panicked because I knew I couldn't go through the forest to get off the cliff, so I tried to climb down."

It takes a moment for Saviel to say anything and when he does; it sounds like he's not entirely buying her story.

"You don't remember how you ended up there?"

"No, I just remember that I had an important message for Seiche, the woman in the cabin."

"What message? You told me you just needed to check on her?"

Aedlin plays with the tips of her fingers, bites her lip. How could she be so careless? How is she supposed to ensure she is keeping Malheim a secret if she can't keep her story straight? Of course, Saviel is going to end up suspicious of her if he catches her out in lies.

"I *did* have to check on her and relay a message. I wasn't going to tell you everything I needed to do. You were a complete stranger, you *are* a complete stranger."

"Whatever the message was could have got the both of us killed. It still could, so don't you think I have a right to know?" Saviel asks, his voice rough and agitated.

"No." Aedlin responds and tucks her knees up to her chest, hugging them against herself tightly.

Aedlin sits quietly, watching the flickering of the fire as her mind runs, the weight of the day settling heavy on her heart.

She needs some way to know that Malheim, that Melody, is okay. Melody never said anything about her not being able to come back. She had to have known what Seiche was going to do to protect them, so she had to have known that Aedlin wouldn't have been able to come home right away. The thought is sobering, but she realises something far more concerning. Something she can't believe it has taken her so long to notice.

"What were you doing on the beach behind the forbidden forest?"

"Sometimes I sail there for the quiet. I came across it once, accidently, and it just became somewhere I find myself going whenever I feel I need it. It didn't take too long to notice that no one else ever seems to go there." He shrugs as he gets up to grab another log, he places it by the fire, ready to add it when the flame dies down.

"You should get some sleep; we still have a long way to go before we reach Khard. With any luck we will make it there late morning the day after tomorrow."

Aedlin's stomach bubbles and growls, Saviel's words repeat over and over in her mind until she is dizzy with the realisation.

"We have to go that long without food?" she asks quietly, somewhat ashamed of her complaining.

"No, there is a small goblin village just a few hours from here. If you have enough gold to hand over, you will usually find a goblin willing to trade some food and drink."

"Goblins?" Aedlin asks, surprised. "Will we be safe? What if they know the guards are looking for us?"

"A lot of the goblins choose to live in the forest

amongst themselves because they wish to keep to their own kind. They don't have trouble with anyone else's business, especially the kings or his men. Assuming they even know about the magic being used, or the fact that it was us, doesn't matter to them. They will be quick to send us back on our way though, so don't expect that we will stop there and rest while we eat." He gets the other log and sets it down on the fire. "Besides, I'm pretty sure the king's men don't even know who they are looking for. If they did, those men we ran into earlier wouldn't have bothered with small talk."

"Yes, I suppose you're right." Aedlin says, followed by a yawn.

"Get some sleep. I will keep watch. I don't suspect anyone will cross our path this late into the night, but I will feel better for the both of us if I make sure."

"Wake me up when you need a break. We will keep watch in shifts." Aedlin mumbles tiredly as she lays down on her cloak.

"That's not necessary. Just sleep." Saviel argues.

"Don't be ridiculous, of course it is. You need to sleep too."

Choosing not to argue further, Saviel agrees to wake her.

CHAPTER FIVE

Aedlin wakes to the sound of someone walking some-where close by her. Leaves crunch under their feet to the left of her face, only a few feet away. Her mind races, trying to come up with some sort of plan of action. Saviel hasn't said anything yet, which only makes her worry grow more. She considers attempting to grab her blade, but she doesn't want whoever it is to see her make the movement.

"Aedlin, wake up." Saviel says from the same area Aedlin had heard the footsteps.

His voice is neutral, giving no sign that anything is

wrong. Trust her to allow herself to get worked up into a state of fear because of Saviel… again.

she opens her eyes and stretches out her aching, stiff limbs. It's hard to pinpoint if the pain is because of all the running yesterday or sleeping on the hard ground- or both.

she jumps up suddenly, making Saviel leap back in surprise.

"Is everything okay?" Saviel asks, concerned.

"It's morning!"

"Yes, it is. How observant of you. Hence why I woke you up. We need to get moving. Make sure you've got everything on you that you need so we can go."

"You didn't wake me up?"

Saviel picks up Aedlin's cloak from the ground, shakes off the dust and passes it to her.

"Put this back on. Keep your head covered and low."

She takes the cloak from him and puts it on.

"Why didn't you wake me up?"

Saviel kicks the ash from the fire around, flattening it out, then kicks some dirt over the top to cover it up, then tosses some leaves over the top.

"I didn't wake you because I needed you rested

enough to handle the rest of the way to Khard. We are as good as dead if you can't keep up."

"You said we wouldn't make it to Khard until the day after tomorrow, right?"

"Right?" Saviel says wearily.

"Tonight, when we stop to rest again, I take the watch shift. No arguments."

"Sure thing." Saviel says as he begins walking, continuing in the direction they had been going before they stopped for the night. Aedlin knows that Saviel's response was sarcastic, but that's an argument she can save for later. Right now, he is right. They need to get moving and get to Khard. As soon as they do, it will be easier for her to separate from him and make her way back home to Malheim.

* * * *

By midday, they reach a part of the forest where the trees aren't as dense against each other. The sun breaks through with ease now and Aedlin's hair is quickly becoming drenched with sweat under her hood.

"Can we stop for water?" she asks, her voice dry and her mouth sticky from dehydration.

Saviel stops and looks takes a quick look around. By the narrowing of his eyes and the way he looks toward their intended path, Aedlin thinks he is going to say no, but then his eyes fall on her. His eyes widen at the sight of her red, sweat-drenched face.

"Yes, of course. Here, give me your cloak, you should take it off, at least while we stop so you can drink. But we won't be able to stay here for long. Especially this exposed in the daylight. We could afford to take that risk in the dark, but not now." He hands Aedlin the canister of water and she gives him her cloak to hold.

"Take a seat over there." Saviel points to a moss-covered log to the right of them and Aedlin does what he says. She sips at the water, fighting everything in herself to not gulp down the whole thing. Instead, after one last sip, she passes it to Saviel.

"Thanks. Here, make sure you have some, too." Aedlin insists.

"No, please, make sure you drink as much as you need. I can have a drink when we find more water." Saviel pushes the water back toward her and she takes one more sip. She gives Saviel a small, thankful smile, then passes it back to him.

Instead of taking it, he tosses her cloak at her, making her drop the water.

92

"Saviel!" she shouts, annoyed.

"Put it on now and keep your head low." He growls.

Aedlin doesn't hesitate. She stands up and quickly puts her cloak back on. She puts the hood on then lowers her head before moving to stand my Saviel's side. She stands close enough that their arms touch. She tries to ignore how the fear that was on the verge of drowning her seems to stifle a little, just with the knowledge that he is so close to her.

Still, even with her feeling safer, she finds herself reaching for her blade.

Saviel slowly reaches down, and grans hold of her wrist.

"Not yet." He whispers in her ear.

She doesn't mean it, but she moves her hand up, so he is holding that instead of her wrist. She expects him to let go, but instead he gives it a quick squeeze. She wishes that the small, caring gesture bought her comfort, but instead it just makes her feel worse. The realisation that he is just as worried as her sends a sharp shiver throughout her entire body.

"Just keep your head low and let me talk with them. If it's the king's men again, I have no choice but to have to talk our way out of this. I will not draw my blade on them unless absolutely necessary."

Horses' hooves trample the ground. The sound of it approaching gets louder and as it does Aedlin finds herself clinging tighter to Saviel.

"That's not right." Saviel says, his voice low and close to her ear.

"What's not, right?" she whispers, keeping her head down.

"There is only one horse. The king's men never travel alone."

"Are you sure?"

"Yes, I'm also sure that the horse is pulling a cart."

"You can tell that just be the way it sounds?"

"Yes." He replies but he doesn't get a chance to say anything else before they have to jump out of the way of a horse pulling an enclosed cart, just as Saviel had said.

Aedlin once again makes an attempt to reach for her blade but is taken by surprise by the sound of someone singing, well at least trying.

The horse stops abruptly and so does the singing.

"Sorry about that, Ma'am, sir. My boy cheddar here hasn't been taken out for a long-distance ride in months. He hasn't slowed once since we left home."

"It's not a problem. No harm done." Saviel reassures

the goblin sitting at the front of the cart.

"You sure? The two of you look rougher than a troll on heat, with nothing to do with his meat." The goblin proceeds to laugh hard enough at his joke that Aedlin is worried he is going to fall from his seat.

"We are fine. Thank you for your concern." Saviel steps closer to the horse and runs his hand along its side. He walks to the front of it and holds his hand under its chin and with the other rubs his hand up and down the length of its snout.

"He's certainly a beautiful creature. What are you using him to transport? Besides yourself, of course."

"Why should I tell you? If you want to know what's in the back of my cart, you're going to have to meet me in Khard and find out like everyone else." The goblin gives Saviel a wink and clicks his tongue. Aedlin would shake her head at him. But she doesn't want to do anything that will draw any attention to herself. She isn't too worried about keeping her head down now that she knows he isn't one of the kings me, but still, she would rather be careful.

"Sure, we could meet you in Khard where you plan on setting up shop making some spiced meat dish or you could take a break from your travels, set up your equipment and share some of your food in exchange for my lips remaining sealed about this horse being one that belongs in King Erevin's stables."

The goblin leans back in his seat and places his right hand under his chin, tapping his first finger on his lips and making a show of thinking over Saviel's request and threat.

"You've got a good nose, elf, but I will have you know I have the papers right here that say that this horse was purchased legally and not at all from the dark elf king." He begins rummaging around somewhere at his feet.

"Don't bother wasting your time pretending to have papers for that horse. We both know you're lying." Saviel says, folding his arms over his chest impatiently.

"Ok fair enough I know when it's time to admit defeat." The goblin gets down from his carriage and holds his hand out for Saviel to shake. Saviel doesn't move keeping his arms wrapped tight around his chest. He glares at the goblin for a few moments, but it doesn't seem to bother him at all in fact he gives a wide smile and instead try stepping to the side and holding his hand out to Aedlin. For some reason this makes Saviel relaxes arms and grabs the goblins attention by holding his hand out for him.

"The name's Gerald." The goblin says keeping his

smile as he shakes Saviel's hand. "Travelling cook but more importantly, soon to be world renowned bard." He continues.

Aedlin makes the decision to remove the hood of her cloak and reveal her face deciding that it's a pretty fair bet to say that the goblin is no threat to them.

As soon as she removes the hood Gerald steps closer to her again and pushes his hand out in a second attempt to shake her hand. She grips his hand in response and shakes it and with a smile tells him her name. his eyes widen and his lips part in surprise. Aedlin's heart rate picks up immediately, but she doesn't break eye contact and waits for him to remove his hand from hers first. He shakes his head a little and seems to dismiss whatever thoughts he has before turning back to the cart.

"Alright then, who's hungry?" Gerald asks and walks around to the back of his cart.

Aedlin's stomach growls loud enough for the both of them to hear and that's all the response the goblin seems to need to pick up his pace and get what he needs from the back of the cart.

Saviel helps by lighting a fire for Gerald to place his pot rack over. Aedlin watches with wide hungry eyes as the goblin prepares a spiced meat Stew. She offers to help him when he starts cutting up the onion's potatoes and carrots, but he denies her help saying that the only one who could ever get this recipe right is him, if she wasn't so hungry, she might have taken offence to his statement, but she was far too hungry to care right now.

Pretty quickly, the surrounding air is filled with the smell of the stew. Her stomach rumbles louder the longer they have to wait to eat. Her cheeks pink with embarrassment, but right as they do, she hears Saviel's stomach doing the exact same thing.

"I better get a move on with this. I'm not sure how much longer you two can last. By the sounds of it, I'm at risk of being eaten before this stew if I don't hurry it up."

The three of them laugh, but the whole time Saviel's eyes never leave Gerald. Aedlin wonders for a fraction of a second if Saviel would really be capable of something like that. With the way that he is looking at the goblin, perhaps he is.

She quickly dismisses the ridiculous thought, knowing that more than likely he is still sizing up whether he can trust Gerald.

"So, what's got you two wondering so deep in the forest?" Gerald asks.

"You first." Saviel says. He tries to make it come off as casual, but there's something in his voice and it would seem that Gerald picked it up too because rather than arguing, which is what Aedlin would have expected, he answers.

"I'm making my way to Khard for the first time. I'm gonna set up a pop-up shop somewhere in the main and sell my spiced meat stew. The two of you get the lucky privilege of being the first ones who are not goblins to taste it."

"we're honoured. Aedlin smiles half meaning it but also half at the point that she could eat spiced bark and say she was honoured if that was offered to her.

* * * *

An hour later, the three of them were sitting by the fire eating straight from bowls that Gerald had come prepared with. To both Aedlin and Saviel's surprise, he even pulls out a loaf of bread for them to pull apart and share. As soon as they finish eating, Gerald looks at them eagerness all over his face and it doesn't take long for Aedlin to realise that he's waiting for them to tell him what they think of his food.

"That was fantastic!" Saviel exclaims, surprising both Aedlin and Gerald. Gerald's surprise is quickly replaced with excitement as he gathers up everyone's bowls and spoons to pack back away into the back of his cart.

Aedlin and Saviel Continue to pick up the last of the bread together while Gerald packs away his cooking equipment.

"You're heading to Khard, you say?" Saviel asks as Gerald takes a seat across from them.

"Yes sir. I hope to open a little shop. A permanent place where food lovers can come, sit and enjoy my cooking for a fair-ish price. Why?"

"Because you were going the wrong way."

Aedlin covers her mouth to hide her quiet laugh. She doesn't mean for it to happen. She's not even sure if she's finding it funny that Gerald is lost or if she's finding this whole situation funny because she has finally cracked. Of course, she could just be in a ridiculously good mood because she's just filled her stomach beyond the point of being full with the most delicious stew she's ever shovelled into her mouth.

"No, I can't be going the wrong way. I got the instructions from a very reputable source."

"Well, I hate to be the one to break it to you, but your source's directions are horse-shit." Saviel shrugs then pops his last bite of bread into his mouth.

Gerald appears lost in thought as he mulls over what Saviel said.

Out of nowhere the silence they all sit in becomes deafening, making Aedlin's ears ring. The only sound that ends up being made to break the suffocating emptiness comes from Cheddar. Aedlin gets up from her place beside Saviel. He reaches out, grasping her wrist, not tight but enough to grab her attention.

"I'm going to see Cheddar." She says, pulling her arm away.

He responds with a nod, then asks Gerald something about where he had travelled from.

Aedlin stands in front of cheddar and does exactly as Saviel had before, stroking the horse's nose and then his cheek when the horse rests his head against her.

"Why cheddar?" Aedlin asks as she steps forward to pet the stallion's neck.

"Hypothetically," Gerald says slowly. "I was going to steal some resources, specifically cheese, more specifically, cheddar. I had heard that one of the most recent farms at the time that the Elf King had taken claim of was also cheese-makers. I needed some for one of my recipes and the ability to purchase any was gone the minute he decided to make that farm part of his kingdom. So, still hypothetical, it didn't go as planned. Things went wrong, and I couldn't get the cheddar, but I was able to steal one of the horses to get away. But they will never have any proof because any time anyone asks what

I stole that day, I can simply say I stole Cheddar."

"Hypothetically, of course." Aedlin laughs and plants a kiss above the horse's nose.

"Of course." Gerald repeats.

"If I was going the wrong way to Khard, what do you say to telling me the right directions so Cheddar and I can be on our way?"

"Absolutely, but it will cost you." Saviel says casually.

Aedlin's attention peeks, and she listens intently, but makes it seem as though she is keeping her attention on the horse.

"I already provided you with food. That's all I have to offer you."

"You could offer us a ride; we need to go to Khard too. For reasons that are of no concern to you."

Gerald appears to mull over Saviel's proposition.

"How about more stew for the road?"

"How about a ride and a reminder that the both of us will keep your *hypothetical* story to ourselves?"

This time Gerald doesn't make a show of taking Saviel's threat into consideration.

"Well then, new best friend, road trip it is." Gerald

takes a seat and grabs the reins. "You can either sit up front with me and Fergus or you can ride in the back."

Saviel sighs and gets up from the log. "I will ride in the front long enough to sketch up some directions. I'm assuming you've got some paper and a writing tool. Then, you will stop the carriage and I will join Aedlin in the back."

"Who is Fergus?" Aedlin asks, her eyes wide at the realisation that perhaps they had allowed themselves to trust Gerald a little too quickly if he had someone else with him this who time and didn't even tell them. More curious than that, Aedlin thought, why would they keep themselves hidden? Why not join them to eat at the very least?

"Fergus is my boy. I rescued him a few months back. Trouble is, he gets an uneasy stomach on the road, so I have to settle him to sleep before we can move."

"You have a child with you? What is wrong with you? Why would you leave him alone, hidden and unfed, while the three of us stuffed out faces?"

Gerald rolls his eyes and nonchalantly bends down to retrieve something from the bag at his feet. Saviel immediately jumps into action, calling out Fergus's name and moving things around in the back of the cart. He tosses something large out and the sudden sound makes Aedlin startle.

"Her, what the heck are you doin' to my stuff?" Gerald yells. He tosses his hand drum to the side and jumps back down from the cart.

Aedlin, surprising herself, grabs Gerald's arm, stopping him from getting in Saviel's way.

"Any sign of him?" Aedlin calls out to Saviel, who has now made his way into the cart.

"Any sign of who?" Gerald asks, annoyed and trying to pull his hand away.

Aedlin tightens her grip on Gerald's arm and with the other hand she leans down and grabs her knife. She makes a show of having the knife and holds it close to Gerald's waist.

"Where is the child?" Aedlin demands, holding the point of the blade against his clothing, but not enough that it would hurt.

"Where is Fergus?" Aedlin demands.

"What? He sits up front with me."

"That doesn't make any sense. We would have noticed a child."

"Just let me go and I will show you." Gerald growls, once again trying to pull his hand away.

"I'm not letting you go. You can show me where he

is, but I am coming with you."

"Fine."

Saviel follows right on the heels of Aedlin and Gerald. "Can you at least let me step up onto the carriage without a knife in my side?"

Aedlin looks at Saviel before answering, who has positioned himself close enough to where Gerald will need to stop up onto the carriage that if he was to try anything stupid, Saviel would be able to reach and grab him immediately.

"Go ahead." Saviel says to Aedlin, as if he knew she was asking if it was a good idea or not. She nods her head in response and pulls the knife away.

Gerald immediately steps up and pulls aside a small dark grey cloth that is sitting on the bench seat. He picks something up, something far too small to be a child, but certainly big enough to be a weapon.

Aedlin and Saviel's thoughts seem to once again match one another. She steps back and tightens her grip on the handle of her blade and Saviel moves back away from the cart, instead positioning himself in front of Aedlin.

She pushes aside her instincts to instead protect him, to do the thing she was relentlessly trained to do every day of the week for as long as she can remember. But now isn't the time. Saviel might be choosing to keep out reasons for being in the forest or going to Khard a secret, but she has far bigger things to keep hidden close to her chest.

With her empty hand, she wraps her fingers around the new, too heavy, too different necklace.

Saviel remains focused completely on Gerald, the muscles in his back and arms tense enough for Aedlin to be able to make out through the cotton on his white shirt. How had she not noticed until this moment that he had removed his tunic? Had he taken it off when they had stopped for the night and accidentally left it behind?

Gerald, moving, catches Aedlin's attention. Confused, she steps forward, trying to get a closer look at the red, white and green item in Gerald's hand.

"What is that?" she asks, stepping forward once more.

"This is Fergus." Gerald says proudly.

Saviel walks away from the both of them, shaking his head.

"It's a fungus?"

"How dare you?" Gerald shouts and holds the fungus close to his chest. "He isn't just some fungus. He is an orphan who I found abandoned when he was no more than just a primordia formation."

"Excuse me for just a moment." Aedlin asks, forcing a polite smile. "Can I speak to you for a minute, please?" Aedlin asks Saviel, who has found his way back over to her. She grips his arm and pulls him back toward the log where they sat to eat.

"We cannot get in that goblin's cart. He is absolutely insane." She tries but fails miserably to whisper.

"Look, I know, but he is our best shot at getting to Khard without detection and much sooner than if we continue on foot."

"Is it really worth it? We've done absolutely fine on foot so far." Aedlin crosses her arms over her chest.

"Sure, besides committing murder." Saviel whispers. "Riding with him really is in our best interest. We have to pass through the mountains that separate Khard from the forest. They are covered in a thick, near constant layer of snow almost year-round. The faster we can travel through there in the clothes we have on our backs, the better." Saviel glances toward Gerald, who is gently rocking the mushroom.

"I will sit up front the entire way while you hide in the back. If we encounter anyone or if Gerald does something unexpected, you stay low and wait for me to come, get you."

CHAPTER SIX

Saviel's eyelids grow heavier by the minute, but he continues to push past it, keeping himself alert by focusing on staying alert and watching their surroundings as they pass them.

He glances down to the seat beside him where the mouldy mushroom sits between him and Gerald. Sighs at the sight of it, annoyed about the amount of time they have already lost because Gerald refused to move the carriage until his mushroom had been sung to sleep. It took three ear piercing songs, all of which were sung loud enough to grab the attention of anyone nearby.

He sighs again and goes back to focusing on their surroundings while he lets his mind wander to the dark-haired mystery of a woman sitting hidden safely in the back of the cart. He wonders about who she is, where she came from, what she was really doing on top of that cliff and why she isn't concerned that her family isn't looking for her. A family that he knows has to come from money, judging by the dress she wears and the gold encrusted hilt of her blade.

His unanswerable questions are quickly replaced with thoughts about her that until this point, he hasn't allowed himself to dwell on. Thoughts of the honey-coloured flecks that show up when the sun hits them in just the right way that sit amongst her otherwise jade eyes.

He thinks of the pink of her lips and the way her smile makes his stomach flutter. And how even when wracked with fear she would rather face her problem with the end of her blade, shaky hands and all than run. He knew getting to Khard faster would shorten their time together. Hell, it's even shorter now that he's sitting up front without her. He wonders if he should ask Gerald to stop. What if she's cold? What if it's damp or things are falling on her? He is sure that if she called out, he would hear her just fine and yet it feels like they are worlds apart, the sickening feeling deep in his gut that seems to come whenever he isn't by Aedlin's side. It came when she made him wait outside the cabin, again when he left to get firewood and now, when he is mere feet away, but she is out of his sight. He shakes his head at himself, and in turn, hopes to shake clear the ridiculous protectiveness he has developed for a stranger he knows nothing about. Not even her family name.

"What's got your head in the clouds?" Gerald asks, Saviel is happy for the distraction, no matter how annoying.

"Just hoping the weather stays clear, at least until we hit the mountains. I know it's no more than wishful thinking to hope we won't face freezing winds at the least once we reach them."

"Are the mountains really that bad? I had heard rumours, but I just assumed it was something other goblins said to deter the desire to leave the forest." Gerald tightens his grip on the reigns, it's a small movement that he doesn't want to draw attention to but Saviel notices and considers that when they hit the base of the mountains it will perhaps be for the best if he takes over control of the cart. He is less clothed than both Saviel and Aedlin making his risk for numerous things, frostbite being the kindest to become a very quick problem. Aedlin won't be happy about being in the back with Gerald, but as annoying as he is, he isn't about to let the poor guy die in the cold.

"Unfortunately for the three of us, those rumours are

very true. I have only had to travel through them twice before, but I'm still here to tell the story." Saviel gives Gerald a light-hearted shrug, he knows it's not as convincing as he had hoped it would be. By the frown that tugs at the edges of his lips.

Saviel places his hand on the goblin's shoulder, giving it a reassuring squeeze.

CHAPTER SEVEN

An hour passes since the warmth from outside had finally begun to fill the inside of the cart. Aedlin had heard Saviel and Gerald discussing the mountains being unforgivingly cold, but she had figured if she tucked herself into a corner and shielded herself with her robe, it wouldn't be so bad. To her dismay, it did little to nothing to shield her from the violent winds that blew through the rattling wooden door. The wind whistled loud enough to *almost* cover the sound of her chattering teeth.

"We've still got a few hours until we reach Khard. Do you need us to stop for a umm… break?" Saviel calls out just loud enough for Aedlin to hear through the wall between them.

"No, I'm all good." She calls back, knowing that by the shyness in his voice he is referring to her needing to relieve herself. Her cheeks warm, probably enough for the both of them, but rather than being annoyed at her embarrassment at such a natural thing, she is grateful for the warmth.

Her eyelids grow heavier by the minute. She hadn't allowed herself to fall asleep when her body wanted nothing more than to do just that when she was too cold to move her fingers. But now that the idea of allowing herself to fall asleep doesn't seem to have the lingering threat of her not waking back up again hanging over her she pulls her cloak tighter around herself, leans her head back against the wall of the carriage and allows the weight of her eyelids win.

* * * *

Aedlin wakes with a startle to Saviel, kneeling down in front of her. His hand is reaching out close to her face. Without a second thought, she grips his wrist, burying her nails deep enough to leave indents in his skin.

"I was just trying to wake you up."

"You can do that without touching me." She snarls

"No, of course, you're right. I didn't mean to startle you; I was just going to move your hair out of your face." He slowly tries to stand up and Aedlin gives his wrist one last warning squeeze before letting him go.

She waits for him to step back completely before allowing herself to get up from the floor of the cart.

She steps out after Saviel and stops as soon as the sun hits the bare parts of her skin. It's warmth, starting on her face, travels quickly over the rest of her and without realising it, she lifts her head, closes her eyes and allows herself to enjoy the feeling of the sun kissing her skin.

"How much longer?" she mumbles. Not opening her eyes.

"Not much, even on foot." Saviel says.

"Well, if that's all you two needs. I have my own reasons for traveling to Khard and I'd like to get started on them sooner rather than later."

Aedlin opens her eyes in time to see Gerald give the two of them a salute paired with an ear-to-ear grin before he jumps back up on his carriage and orders cheddar to move.

Aedlin and Saviel watch as Gerald and Cheddar disappear into the trees ahead of them.

"Alright, this is it. There's about an hour's left of travel through some more forest left before we hit the Outer regions of Khard." Saviel says with a relieved but tired smile.

"I couldn't be more ready if I tried. First thing I'm doing when we get there is finding somewhere to sleep with a half decent bed. Actually, scratch that. I'll take a hay filled mattress on the floor at this point. Anything has to be better than spending another night on the Cold ground." Aedlin Responds. Once again, pulling her cloak tight around her shoulders.

They barely break the tree line before Saviel, who had nervously been playing with his fingers while they were walking, turns towards Aedlin.

"So? You really don't remember how you ended up on That Cliff? Not a single thing about who could have put you there. Or how you could have wondered There yourself?"

"No, I still don't remember anything." Aedlin says quickly. And increases the pace of her steps.

He says nothing else but catches up to her pace. And Aedlin closes her eyes, relieved.

"I see it, you know." Saviel murmurs.

"See what?" Aedlin asks, sounding dismissive, but her breath catches in her throat.

"The way your shoulders drop, and you stop holding your breath every time I decide to drop a question that I can see, is making you uncomfortable."

Aedlin becomes very aware of her held breath and makes a show of releasing it. "I'm sure it's just a coincidence. You are reading far too much into something that isn't really there." She shrugs. "Have you noticed whether I do these things when you're not asking me personal questions?"

"Well, no. I suppose not." He mumbles.

"I thought as much." Aedlin says, clicking her tongue disapprovingly. Saviel frowns. It's only a little, and he turns his head away from Aedlin, but not fast enough. She still catches it, and it sends her mind reeling into a dizzy mess of questions. The most important being how and why would he be paying so much attention to her subtle emotional changes? She understands, of course, that she is keeping something huge from him and she is obviously doing a terrible job of lying to him about her memory. But why is he caring enough to notice? And why does she care so much that she has obviously hurt his feelings?

She nudges his shoulder; the move is unexpected, and it makes him stumble. He looks at her, confused at first, but his gaze falls to her apologetic smile and, as soon as it does, he smiles in return. A make your stomach clench, weak on your knees, dizzy kind of smile.

"How much longer did you say?" Aedlin asks, clearing her throat and trying to shove away the overpowering desire to make sure she gets to spend the rest of her life, making him smile like that, just so she can see it.

"Not much further." he says casually, nodding slightly toward the direction they are heading.

CHAPTER EIGHT

"It's beautiful." Aedlin accidentally whispers. A marble castle sits high and mighty, looking down on Khard below that expands as far as she can see. She thought her own home and the castle she had grown up in had been of impressive size, she thought her kingdom, had to have been one of the biggest of all the cities she had heard of from the stories she was told as a child, a sobering realisation hits her heart. They are nothing. If there was ever an invasion of her home from a kingdom like this fae-kind wouldn't stand a chance.

"Not sure that's the word I would use, loud maybe.

It's certainly convenient. I agree the castle is impressive to look at, but Khard itself is… unspectacular."

"I didn't take you for someone who is so negative." Aedlin remarks with a raised eyebrow.

"I said the castle was impressive." he replies with a shrug.

Aedlin looks over Khard as the late afternoon sun sets over it. The golden light covers it like a blanket and, rather than continuing on, she sits in place, watching as the light slowly moves down the castle walls.

"Are you okay? Are you tired?" Saviel asks, dropping quickly to his knees by her side.

"Yeah, it's just, I never thought I would ever get to see anything like this."

A puzzled look crosses Saviel's face as he looks from Aedlin toward Khard, then back at Aedlin.

"You've never been here before?"

"No, I haven't. Is that really so surprising? I'm sure there are plenty of people out there who have never been to Khard."

"Not many." he says, raising his eyebrow.

"Well, I guess I'm just part of that, not many." she shrugs to play it off but just like every other time so far, she knows Saviel is sceptical.

"Do you have time to get something to eat before you have to do whatever it is you have to do?"

Aedlin hesitates, she's already spent so much time away from her kingdom, from Melody and from every other fae who she should have been with from the very beginning, reassuring them, defending them, fighting right by their side. she doesn't have the time to waste, she should have been staying close to Malheim. How could she stomach going to eat a hot meal with Saviel when for all she knows her kingdom is in ruin? She has no reason to believe that Seiche's spell didn't work just as she said it would. But she also has no way of knowing if it did. No, she needs to get back. She's given it enough time, just as Seiche had asked. Well, it will have been enough, she hopes, by the time she returns. If they were going to be caught for Seiche using her magic, they would have by now.

"That's really nice of you to offer, but I think here is where we say goodbye and I say thank you for all of your help and for getting me here." Aedlin says, getting to her feet.

"Oh. But that woman must have told me to bring you here for a reason." Saviel says, also getting back to his feet, looking everywhere but at Aedlin.

"So, are you ready to tell me what your plan is now? Maybe I could help."

His voice is quiet and Aedlin gets a weird feeling in her gut, a tight feeling that doesn't hurt, but it makes her want to throw up. She allows herself a minute to take him in. She dares, for just a moment, to push everything she is worried about and cares about to the side and makes sure she taken in enough of him to hold the memory of his face for as long as possible. She knows that as soon as she is back home, that's it. There is no chance of her ever-seeing Saviel again. But then her thoughts change to what he said about Seiche wanting her to be here. There has to have been a reason, unless it was just to get her as far away from Malheim as possible.

"Maybe I could use something to eat before I continue on." The words are out before Aedlin can take them back, but with the way Saviel's face lights up, she couldn't take it back even if she wanted. He noticed his own reaction and quickly straightens himself up, clears his throat and gives Aedlin a shy smile.

Aedlin, suddenly feeling irrationally shy at the realisation that Saviel might not want to leave her yet, looks down at her fidgeting hands. Her nails are black, filled with the dirt from sleeping on the ground.

"You know what, I could actually use a freshen up. Do you know anywhere I could do that?"

"It just so happens the place I was going to take you to eat also has rooms, most of which have bathrooms. I would be happy to pay for a room for the night for you, even if you only use the room to bathe. You have no obligation to spend the night if you don't want to."

The idea sounds more inviting to Aedlin that she would like to admit, including spending the night in a bed, if she's lucky enough it will even have a half-way decent pillow.

"That sounds perfect." She says with a grateful smile.

* * * *

The sounds and smells coming from the market stalls and storefronts as soon as they hit Khard centre are overwhelming to Aedlin's senses, but she takes in every inch of it. Her heart swells with pride and wonder at the sight of so many races working side by side, some together, others trading goods with each other or just sharing friendly conversation.

"Is it always like this here?" she asks Saviel, who doesn't seem to share the same excitement as her.

"Huh"? he responds, not hearing her properly over the sound of a merchant yelling about the sale he is having on some locally grown fruit she has never heard of.

"Is it always like this here?" She repeats. "Everyone

working and living alongside each other, no matter their race." She clarifies, noticing his confused raised eyebrow.

"Yeah, that's the whole point of this city. It's one of the few places left anywhere near here where absolutely everyone, with the exception of the dark elf King and his followers are allowed."

"How do they enforce it; we didn't pass anyone on our way in to verify us in any way."

"There is no need." He says with a shrug. "The King has this place whole warded against them."

"Magic?" Aedlin stops, grabbing Saviel's arm to get him to stop too. "But how?

"It's disappearing, the magic, but it's not gone yet, and he has promised that he will do everything he can to uphold the ward until there isn't enough magic left to do it."

"That's... kind of him. I hadn't expected to come across such big hearted, kind people, let alone so many of them, let alone again, a king."

He doesn't get a chance to respond before Aedlin turn quickly towards a store behind them. Her nose fills with the smell of tea and suddenly she is very aware of the cool chill biting at exposed parts of her skin. She pulls her cloak tight around her and takes another deep breath.

Taking in the floral scent of tea and honey.

"Come on." Saviel says, grabbing Aedlin's hand.

"Where are we going?" she says, surprised by the carefree giggle that bubbles up from inside.

He leads her over to the store, stopping at a table out the front with only two chairs tucked into it. He lets go of her hand and pulls one of the seats out.

"Wait here."

"Aedlin opens her mouth to protest, or at the very least, tell him what tea she likes but he doesn't give her the chance. He is already back turned and walking into the little store.

Aedlin takes the quiet moment she has to herself and allows herself the opportunity to take in everything around her. Her whole life she has known nothing but her own kingdom and the people within it. Not having any idea that just outside its boundaries has been a whole other world, bustling with people with lives, different kingdoms, cities and most surprising of all, different races. While she watches the guy with the fruit stand exchange some produce with a female elf with white as snow hair that she has braided on either side of her face. She dons a stunning corset dress bluer than the ocean she had sailed on to get here. She finds herself unable to stop from wondering if she could put a stop to hiding away her kingdom, she could show everyone just how truly beautiful the world outside the walls of Malheim are. Just as soon as she really lets herself consider just how perfect of an idea it would be, being able to open up to more trade partners, allow the children of Malheim to know more than just a life lived in captivity; the reality of the situation crumbles around her. She could never let her kingdom be free from its protective walls, not while the dark elf king, her father is still alive. The answer is clearer now than it has even been, she had no clue what it would take to run a kingdom before, but now she is starting to get an idea of what it is really going to take… she has to kill her father, to free her kingdom.

"Is everything alright?" Saviel asks as he places two teacups on sauces down on the table with a couple of sugar cubes and spoons.

"Yes, of course. Why wouldn't it be?" she asks, taking one of the cups of tea and bringing it to her lips.

"You just seemed lost in thought." he replies and adds two of the sugar cubes to his tea. They sit in silence while Saviel stirs the sugar in and Aedlin continues to take in the sounds of Khard.

"Saviel!" the elf who was purchasing fruit from the merchant calls out. "Is that you?"

Saviel turns his head at the sound of his name and the elf rushes toward him.

"Eleise?" Saviel gets up from the table and opens his arms. His face lights up. The tiny elf is almost lost in Saviel's arms as they hold each other tightly.

Aedlin sinks down in her chair, feeling irrationally embarrassed.

"Where have you been? Laurie has been looking all over for you!"

"Why?" Saviel steps back from Eleise. Every one of his back muscles seems to tense in an instant.

Eleise leans in close, ignoring that Saviel is trying to step back again. She speaks low enough for Aedlin to not be able to hear.

Saviel looks back at Aedlin for just a moment, but just as quickly, he turns back and immediately shakes his head. And appears to wave off whatever has just been said about Aedlin.

They continue to speak in hush tones and Aedlin, although still curious, allows herself the distraction of the merchants again.

"It will be your head, Saviel, and I won't be there to save you this time. I will never understand why it's always you who ends up tangled in others' mess all the time." Eleise shouts. This time, it's her turn to step back from Saviel.

"I *just* told you I have no idea about the magic that was reported. How could I? I was nowhere near any beach, let alone a cottage on a beach."

"You are a terrible liar, Saviel Freighn, and a damned fool."

"It's always nice running into you, Eleise." Saviel calls out to the elf's back as she hurriedly walks away.

He sits back down at the table and gulps down the entirety of his tea, with no reaction qt all to how hot it still is.

"You finished?" Saviel says sharply. His voice is grave and his eyes narrow.

"No, I'm not finished. But if you have somewhere you need to be, please go. Don't stay on my behalf." Her words are genuine, but she can't help the disappointment she knows she will feel if he says yes, and she no longer has the option for a wash and rest.

Saviel runs his hands through his hair and sighs loudly. His eyes bear into Aedlin's, the dust meeting the grass. Time passes slowly and they are both completely aware of the hold they have on each other and yet, neither seems to want to, or is able to, let go. Aedlin's shoulders tense at the same moment that Saviel's relaxes.

A vender calls out nearby about his fruit and the sudden sound seems to be enough to break whatever it was that was keeping them in place.

"No, I promised you a place to bathe and sleep, and I intend to keep that promise. I apologise for my forgotten manners. Please, finish your tea." Saviel says quietly. Distracted, but seemingly sincere.

Saviel sits patiently across from Aedlin and watches quietly as she finishes her drink, occasionally giving an appreciative hum after a sip and taking in the surrounding everything.

"Are you sure everything is alright?" Aedlin asks, placing down her empty cup.

"Nothing that I need to concern myself with right now."

"But she mentioned the magic Seiche used?"

"It's nothing. We should get a move on; we don't want to risk the chance of no rooms being available." He gets up quickly and this time Aedlin does the same.

"Do you live here in Khard?" Aedlin asks as they pass the market fronts and further away from the painstakingly cold of the mountains.

"No." Saviel says seemingly casually, but his lack of elaboration catches Aedlin off guard.

"I just assumed because of you knowing where I can spend the night."

He doesn't say anything further and Aedlin struggles to keep her curiosity at bay. She tries to distract herself by looking into the storefront windows. They pass a bakery, and the smell of freshly baked bread sends a wave of warmth from her heat to her feet.

Saviel turns to Aedlin, noticing that she was no longer keeping pace with him.

"Sorry." She says with an embarrassed smile.

He shakes his head and smiles back at her.

"Come on." He says, once again grabbing her hand.

He leads her into the bakery and points to the display of various fresh baked loaves. She practically starts drooling at the sight of the different fruit breads, nut breads, seeded loaves with various fungus types looking like it's growing from the top.

"What type of bread is that?" Aedlin says with her nose scrunched up in disgust.

"You bake it using fast-growing spores. Within an hour, the fungus is sprouting through the top of the bread. It's a favourite among most goblins."

"Mornin" a large man in white cloth clothes and a white apron says from behind the counter. His hands are covered in flour and, curiously, so are parts of the top of his bald head.

"Morning." Saviel says with a nod.

"Can I help you folk with anything in particular to-day?"

"Yeah, she'd love a fruit loaf, plain white and what-ever you've got that's covered available that's covered in cinnamon." Saviel says without so much as a look over to Aedlin to make sure she actually wanted anything he had said.

"Sure thing." The baker replies before rushing around behind the display and packing up Saviel's order.

Aedlin opens her mouth to protest but decides against it. It would feel awfully rude to protest something he is purchasing with his own money.

Saviel exchanges the bread and money with the baker, thanks him and then leaves. Aedlin follows closely be-hind, also giving the baker a quick "thank you" on her way out.

"A little something to pair with the soup I plan on or-dering when we get to the tavern." He says, holding up the paper wrapped bread.

"Perfect." Aedlin says, her stomach grumbling in agreeance.

They walk a few more blocks along the market strip, Aedlin keeps her pace casual as she returns the mostly all friendly greeting from merchants attempting to get their attention and attract them to purchase from them. Saviel and Aedlin lose step with each other multiple times, Saviel walking ahead but slowing back down every time he realises Aedlin is not right to be on his side. If her walking so slowly is bothering him, he doesn't let it show, in the face of his shoulders appear to be the most relaxed they have been since they met and his occasional glances toward her are always paired with a small but genuine smile.

"Down here." Saviel says and directs her down an alley way. They follow the narrow alley lined with the back of stores and some occasional small homes before making another turn down another narrow street. This one almost immediately smells and feels different. There is the stench of stale beer hanging thick in the air. Someone down a nearby side street curses immediately followed by the sound of glass shattering from the same direction.

"Saviel?" Aedlin mutters.

"Don't worry, they are little rough, and sometimes so are the people who like to hang out here, but you won't find a better home cooked feed unless it was made by your own mother, assuming she knows how to cook." He gives her a wink, but it does nothing to dull the anxiousness sitting heavy in her.

"Right through here." He says, directing her done one last bend before stopping out the front of a tavern. Music and chatter spill out from inside, mixed with the smell of ale and food.

Saviel once again grabs hold of Aedlin's hand. He gives it a reassuring squeeze and, to Aedlin's surprise, leans down, drops the loaves of bread on the floor and uses his other hand to tuck a loose strand of hair behind her ear.

she intends to lean back, to force his hand away from hers but instead she stays, she drowns in the dark of his eyes, not coming back up for air until she realises that he is smiling at her leaning into his hand. The sudden warmth in her cheek's spreads all throughout her body. She clears her throat and steps back but keeps hold of his hand.

"You ready to get something to eat?" he asks while picking the bread back up.

"More than ever."

"Good."

The both of them enter through the door of the tavern, Saviel leads Aedlin across the length of the room and pulls out one of the seats that are situated at the bar for her to sit on.

"Olive!" he calls out to the woman behind the bar

who's back is facing them.

She turns at the call of her name and Aedlin's eyes widen at the sight of her.

Her blonde locks fall over her breasts that overflow from the top of her dress, pushed up by a corset that sits tight around her waist. Her larger physique shapes her in all the right places, enough so that Aedlin finds herself blushing at the realisation that she has been staring.

Her lips are plump and cherry red with lipstick, her cheeks pink with a light dusting of blush, and her large blue eyes stand out against her fair skin.

Aedlin forces herself to put her attention toward the selection of bottles behind Olive.

"Saviel!" she exclaims excitedly.

She immediately turns back around and grabs a bottle of something from behind her and a mug.

"Two please." Saviel says, holding up two fingers.

"Oh?" Olive responds. She looks at Aedlin and realises that is who Saviel must be talking about.

"Sure." she says, grabbing another mug.

"I'm okay, actually." Aedlin says politely but not loud enough for either of them to hear over the sound of the full tables behind them, occupied by either drunk, or those on their way to being drunk.

Olive pours them both a drink and Aedlin accepts it with a smile. Not wanting to tell her no now that she has already placed it in front of her.

"Are you in town for long?" Olive asks Saviel.

"Long enough to need to book a room for the night if you have anything available? Two rooms."

"Two? You won't be sharing with your friend?" she asks, raising her eyebrow and looking at Aedlin.

Saviel coughs, splattering some of his drink across the bar.

"She's not that type of friend, Olive."

Aedlin wraps her hands tighter around the mug and looks down at it, refusing to look back up at either of them, worried that if she does, she won't be able to do it with a straight face.

"My mistake. Yeah, I've got a couple of rooms available, assuming you're good for it." She gives Saviel a wink and holds out her hand.

"Do you really think I would do you dirty like that? Of course, I'm good at it." Saviel reaches into a pocket inside pocked and pulls out a coin satchel. To Aedlin's surprise, he hands her the whole satchel.

"Take what you need for the two rooms, these drinks plus at least two more and let's just assume we will need dinner later than well as the lunch we came here for."

Olive winks at Saviel and takes the satchel. She turns back to the shelf behind her and pours the money from the bag and begins counting it out, separating what she needs.

The door bursts open behind them, Aedlin startles but doesn't look back at the commotion. She notices that neither does Saviel, but Olive does give a quick glance back over her shoulder.

"I'm tellin' ya. If we go in ocean side before dawn, we could infiltrate the walls of that arsehole's castle." One of them says, their voice slurred."

"Sure, we could Deon." One of the others says sarcastically.

"We could!" he continues, yelling defensively now. "We could separate, slip through the castle undetected, and the first one to find him, asleep or otherwise, is the one who gets to draw their blade to his throat."

Saviel chuckles to himself as he shakes his head.

"Ya, find something funny?" one of the men calls out.

Saviel doesn't respond. Just picks up his mug and takes a drink from it.

"Hey Olive, would you mind grabbing us both a bowl of soup please?"

"Sure thing." Olive says slowly. She gives Saviel a side glance and a wave of nervousness washes over her face. Aedlin notices it, but Saviel either doesn't seem to or chooses to ignore it.

Heavy boots pound against the wooden floor, closing the distance between them and the men.

Aedlin looks at Saviel with wide eyes, her mouth falls open when all he does is smirk up at her.

The footsteps get closer, and she pulls her hood lower over her face. She leans down over her drink and grips the mug so tightly that the skin over her knuckles goes white.

Aedlin glances to the side the best she can to see Saviel, surely, he is going to get them both out of there, or maybe he won't maybe she needs to get out of here herself and leave him to deal with the results of his carelessness. Honestly, why should she stick around? He is the one who thought it was a wise decision to laugh at a drunk buffoon talking about a big game. He thinks he could take on the dark elf king, her father. She shudders at the thought. Of course, especially in a drunken state, he is going to see Saviel as no more than a mere inconvenience that he could no doubt have on the floor in record time, assuming he does have some clue about how to fight someone.

Aedlin settles on the decision to leave him to his business before she can change his mind in just enough time to feel someone standing directly behind her.

She squares her shoulders, takes a sharp breath and gets to her feet. When she turns, she is face to face with five men... well, one man, an orc, two elves and a dwarf.

"My, you're a pretty thing." The human says his voice matching that of the one who was planning to take out the elf king.

"Don't you think she's pretty Malo?" he purrs, running his tongue along his bottom lip.

"Pretty enough to take a bite out of." The oark responds, his deep, gravelly voice is right in the pit of Aedlin's stomach, and her panic filled chest begins to rapidly rise and fall.

"Sorry gentlemen, this one's spoken for. Why don't you lot find yourselves a seat and enjoy some good food and drink with the rest of us?" through gritted teeth and a plastered-on smile.

He slips his arm through Aedlin's and pulls her closer to him. The man in front of them looks at them, unconvinced, and she leans her weight into Saviel in an attempt to sell it more that they really are together.

"What's that 'round her neck?" the dwarf asks and immediately the man's eyes fall to the necklace hanging around Aedlin's chest.

"It's nothing," she says quickly. "Just something I made. It's not worth anything."

"I think I'll be the judge of that." He says and reaches a hand out toward Aedlin and the necklace.

Aedlin's breath hitches in her throat as panic sets in. She can't let him take it. The minute he does her life and everyone still in Malheim will be in danger. Her hands begin trembling as she races to figure out what to do, but it's too late. In a split second, his hand is on the necklace; she unhooks her arm from Saviel and puts both of her hands out to push the man away. Everyone who was standing around her hits the ground as she does. She starts to get up, but something slams onto her back, forcing her back down. She cries out in both pain and shock from the unexpected force before once again trying to get up, and get whatever is on her back, off.

"Stay down!" A familiar voice whisper-shouts in her ear.

"Gerald?"

"Yes, it's me. Stay down and stay quiet!"

She does as he says while trying to discreetly feel if her necklace is still in place. To her horror, it isn't. right at that same moment, it feels as though Gerald adjusts her cloak and she realises that he is trying to keep her hidden, but that means he saw her. Can she trust him enough to keep this to himself? How could she let this happen? Why didn't she run instead of entertaining a conversation with them?

"Gerald? What the hell are you doing? Get off!" Saviel shouts at Gerald.

Gerald doesn't say anything, but he must have signalled to Saviel to get down.

Aedlin turns her head away from him. She cannot let anyone else see.

"Gerald, I need the necklace!" she whispers in a panic.

"What?"

"The necklace he ripped off my neck. I need you to get it."

"Yes, right now. I need it."

"Right, stay down. I will be right back." His voice is sceptical, but he gets up.

"Are you hurt?" Saviel asks as soon as Gerald is off her back.

"No, I'm alright." She whispers, still refusing to look at him.

Gerald rushes back over to Aedlin and hands the

necklace to her. She scrambles to untangle it and get it back on, but she quickly notices that the clasp is broken. She yells out in frustration and both Saviel and Gerald hover closer to her.

"What's wrong?" Gerald asks, his concern seeming to match her own.

"It's broken!"

"What does that mean?"

"It means give me the necklace and get her the hell upstairs and into one of the rooms, I will join you as soon as I can." Olive says from somewhere beside her.

Aedlin and Gerald both stay in place, neither of them sure if that is such a good idea.

"Now, before they come to!" she yells at them.

They scramble to their feet, Aedlin continues to keep her head -and hood low as she rushes to put on the necklace her mother had gifted her that she had been keeping in her pocket.

"The rest of ya, mind ya business, and get back to drinking."

Aedlin hadn't noticed how completely silent the tavern had gotten until everyone went back to nervously chattering amongst themselves.

"Is someone planning on telling me what is going on?" Saviel asks.

"Not until you lead those two upstairs and show them where the rooms are." Saviel tries to say something else, but Olive doesn't give him the opportunity.

"Now Saviel!" she shouts and gives him a shove.

CHAPTER NINE

"Does anyone want to tell me what in the world is going on?" Saviel asks, panicked and pacing back and forth in front of the bed where Aedlin and Gerald sit.

"Saviel, can you please just sit? Your pacing isn't helping." Aedlin whispers through her hands as she holds against her face.

"Sit? How am I supposed to sit? How are *you* just sitting? Saviel asks, waving a hand towards Gerald.

Aedlin keeps her head low and her wings as tight

against her back as she can. She lowers her left hand, letting go of the wings that hang back in their rightful place around her neck. Having a handful of others know who she really is has a mountain of risks, even if she is eighty percent sure Saviel isn't *likely* to betray her. That still leaves others who she knows nothing about. Part of her wants to breathe a sigh of relief that her big secret that she has been keeping from Saviel is now out. But it would be foolish of her to think that her identity being out is enough to let go of the weight she is carrying on her, almost broken under the pressure of shoulders. She still has to keep the location and existence of the rest of Malheim a secret.

"Saviel, I need you to breathe. I need to know that you can handle what you saw, and I need to know I can trust you to keep it to yourself."

He stops pacing and turns to face the both of them.

He closes the space between them and kneels in front of Aedlin, grabbing hold of both of her hands and holding them securely in hers.

"You might have many things to worry about right now Aedlin, but I promise you, me betraying you is not one of them."

"Same here." Gerald says, placing his hand over Saviel's.

Aedlin shakes her other hand free of Saviel's and places it on top of Gerald's, giving it a squeeze.

Saviel pulls his hand away and gets back to his feet.

"What do we do?" he asks quietly.

"I need to know who, if anyone, saw me."

Saviel looks to the door, then back to Aedlin.

"Right, I'm going to find out. Maybe Olive already knows. What am I supposed to do if someone did see you?"

"I honestly have no idea." Aedlin sighs.

Saviel's eyebrows narrow as he grips the door handle.

"Gerald, would you mind giving us a moment? There is something I need to discuss with Aedlin in private."

Gerald hesitates, looking from Aedlin to Saviel quietly with wide eyes.

"It's alright." Aedlin says, giving Gerald's hand another squeeze.

Gerald hesitantly gets up from the bed and crosses the room to Where Saviel is still standing in front of the door.

Saviel lowers his hand from the door handle and steps to the side, out of Gerald's way.

"I just need a few minutes." Saviel says in an attempt to reassure an obviously concerned Gerald.

"Mhmm" Gerald responds before leaving the room.

"What is it that you need to talk about?" Aedlin asks as soon as Saviel faces her.

Saviel runs his hands through his hair and refuses to meet Aedlin's gaze.

"Saviel, really, what is it?"

"It's probably nothing. I'm sure I was just imagining things in the moment of chaos." He lowers his hands from his hair and shakes his head as if he is trying to shake away something he is seeing.

Aedlin's breath catches in her throats as she suspects she knows exactly what Saviel is going to ask her. He saw *her,* the *real* her behind the protection of her necklace.

She gets to her feet and closes the space between them until she is so close that his warm breath makes her fine hairs stand on end when his breath connects with her skin.

"Ask me." She whispers.

"I don't think I should."

"Ask me." She repeats.

He hesitates for two… three seconds. His eyes finally meet hers and he holds the both of them in place, keeping his eyes locked with hers as he lets the question spill out.

"Did I really see that parts of your skin were blue while you were on the ground?"

Aedlin does her best to not let her emotions waver in any way. Her mind rushes chaotically through scenarios of what would happen if she chose to tell him that he didn't imagine what he saw, or that he did. She could continue to lie to him. She doesn't owe him the truth any more than she has already given him, both accidentally and on purpose. But he has shown time and time again that he has given her no reason to continue lying to him. There is something within the brown of his eyes that grips her entirely and wraps her in it's warm, safe embrace. Part of her wants to let herself succumb to it, to melt into the safety that his eyes seem to promise, a safety that feels just the same as Malheim used to bring.

"Aedlin?" Saviel's voice is low, on the brink of a desperate growl, and it's her undoing. In a movement so swift it makes Saviel stumble back half a step Aedlin locks the door, grabs Saviel's hand and as an extra protective measure to ensure no other eyes will see what she is about to show him she grabs his hand and leads him to the small bathroom to the left of the room. She closes and latches the door once they are both inside.

"What is going on?" he asks wide eyed.

Aedlin takes a deep breath and once again positions herself in front of him, this time not as close, but still because of the bathroom, they are suddenly too close for her comfort by taking into account she has no way of knowing how he is going to react to what she is about to show him.

"I need you to not overreact, I need you to remember the version of me you have gotten to know over the last couple days, I need you to know I love the feel of the spring air against my face, I need you to know that I think there has never been a greater food invented then cheese cake and I need you to know that I am good, I adore children, I love those who I care about ferociously and I would give the last of everything I have to someone who needed it more."

"Aedlin, honestly, you're starting to scare me. Please, just tell me what is going on. Whatever it is, I'm sure it can't be that bad."

Aedlin reaches behind her neck. She closes her eyes and once again takes a breath. She locates the clasp, grips it and, with shaky hands, undoes it.

She opens her eyes as she lowers the necklace, dropping it into her left hand and closing her fist tight around it.

Saviel opens his mouth to say something, but nothing comes out. He just stands there, frozen, watching motionless as Aedlin's appearance once again changes right before his eyes.

"Saviel?" Aedlin says quietly, testing the waters and trying to gage something from him.

"You're… you're a dark elf." He chokes the words out, his mouth remaining open, gaping at her.

"I'm half dark elf." She corrects, knowing as soon as she said it that it really doesn't matter, not when the dark elves, especially her father are *the* most hated race across all of Agoura.

"Saviel, please say something." She pleads and reaches her right hand out to him.

To her surprise he coils away from her. He steps back until his back is against the door, appearing to be trying to put as much distance between them as he can.

"How could you not tell me?" He spits, the disgust on his face matches his voice, and her stomach sinks.

"I couldn't tell you. I had to hide that I'm a fae. That information was dangerous enough on its own. Of course, I couldn't tell you the truth about *also* being a dark elf."

He refuses to look at her or say anything. Aedlin tries

once more to step closer to him, but he holds his hand up.

"Stop." He growls and turns quickly, unlatching the lock, then leaving her standing alone in the bathroom in a deafening silence.

The other door opens, then promptly slams shut. The sudden sound makes her startle, but she still remains frozen in place. Her mind is reeling with regret and having to come to terms with the completely reckless and stupid mistake she has made. She knew better than to allow him to know who she really was. She knew better than to have him know she was a fae. She drops to the ground and cries out. How could she have gotten this all so wrong? How can she be expected to keep her home and everyone in it safe and hidden, well as hidden as they still can be now that their borders have already been infiltrated? She wipes her face clean and the sound of the patrons in the bar below pulls her back out of her pity pool.

She snaps herself back together, quickly fastens the necklace back in place, and rushes out of the bathroom. She scoops her cloak up from the bed and throws it on before rushing out of the room.

She looks down over the railing to the bar below to see if she could spot Saviel.

"What are you doing? You need to get back inside!" Gerald yells from the flight of stairs to her right.

"Where is Saviel?" She asks frantically, continuing to look down at the bar.

"He left. I thought he was doing something to help you. Whatever his reason for leaving was important enough for him to shove someone out of his way and not even take a second to look back and apologise."

Aedlin slams her hand down on the railing and sucks in a sharp breath to keep herself from cussing.

She turns on her heel and goes back into the room, slamming the door behind her. She sits down on the bed, picks up the pillow, brings it to her face and screams into it. A loud, soul emptying scream that quickly turns into heart aching sobs.

"What's happened?" Gerald asks.

"Please, just leave me alone." She pleads, not caring if Gerald can hear her muffled voice or not.

"Aedlin, get yourself together. If you don't know where Saviel is, we need to go find him."

Aedlin lowers the pillow from her face. She notices but ignores the tear stains on it and places it down beside her.

"We don't need to go find him. Even if we do, he isn't coming back."

"Why, what happened?"

"It… it doesn't matter." Aedlin says, getting up from the bed and going to the bathroom.

Gerald says something else, but Aedlin can't make out what it is over the sound of the running water she uses to rinse off her tear-stained face.

"Aedlin, you're gonna' have to tell me what's going on. Why would he just run out like that?"

"He's spooked about me being a fae." She says dismissively, not willing to let her secret out to *anyone* else, and turns off the water.

"Well, of course he is. I am too, but you don't see me running away. I mean, obviously we can't tell anyone about you. We can't risk *him* telling anyone."

"Why do you think I'm looking for him?"

The door opens again and Gerald signals for Aedlin to stay where she is and raises his finger to his lips to tell her to stay quiet. He leaves the bathroom and only seconds later returns.

"It's alright, it's the bartender."

Aedlin lets go of the breath she had been holding and leaves the bathroom once more.

"I have something for you." Olive says and holds out Aedlin's other necklace.

"Thank you so much!" Aedlin squeals and practically

dives for the necklace.

She rushes back to the bathroom to privately swap the necklaces back over.

"There is something we need to talk about." Olive says as Aedlin comes back out.

"Look, I have somewhere I need to be. Thank you so much for fixing my necklace and for your help. I appreciate it more than I can say." She double checks she still has her dagger and the necklace she just put in her cloak pocket. She puts her hood back and barely gets to take a step when Olive grabbed her arm as she tries to leave.

"You can't go anywhere." Olive says.

Aedlin immediately recoils away from her touch and glowers at her, but rather than letting go, she tightens her grip.

"It's not safe for you to leave."

"That's not for you to decide. Now let go."

Gerald reaches up and puts his hand over Olive's.

"She asked you to let go." He smiles, but his eyes are narrowed.

This time she lets go, but positions herself in front of the door.

"Look, I agree that it's a risk for her to leave, but you

can't just keep her held hostage in here." Gerald says crossing his arms.

"Actually, I can. I have already sent for the King to be notified that you are here."

"You what?" Aedlin reaches for her dagger and narrows her eyes.

"Now, now, there's no need for that. I'm on your side. You need to be somewhere safe; the castle is the safest place in the kingdom."

Aedlin grits her teeth together. "Isn't that something I should get to decide?" Aedlin snaps, gripping the hilt tighter.

"Perhaps so, but we didn't have the time to discuss it. It will take the King no more than a few hours to have someone here to collect you."

Aedlin looks at Gerald in the hopes that he would have a way for her to get out of this, but he just shrugs art her apologetically.

She can't be taken to someone else's castle; she should be on her way back to her own... Or her fathers, she hasn't figured that out yet, after all how is she supposed to risk her life by confronting her father who will most likely have her killed when Melody will be expecting her back and the rest of Malheim needs her?

Although perhaps the King will be happy to let her return home, not that she would tell him where that *actually* is. Saviel had mentioned that the King was a good man and Olive really does have a point about the castle being the safest place she could be.

"Fine." she finally says and puts her dagger away.

Olive breathes a sigh of relief, and her shoulders appear to un-tense.

"Thank you for accepting that I am just trying to help." Her smile is warm and seems genuine, but Aedlin knows better than to let her guard down around her.

"Right, I'm going to go get you that soup you were waiting for. Saviel already paid for two serving and he still ain't back, so I will just bring the other bowl up for you." She nods at Gerald quickly leaves.

"I need you to go find Saviel."

"Now?" Gerald asks, his tone whiny.

"Yes now, please. This is important."

"But she's going to get me soup."

"Gerald, please!" she pleads with him.

"Fine, but you need to look after Fergus for me. It's been a long day and I want him to rest."

He pulls Fergus out of his pocket and Aedlin's mouth

falls open.

"I... I don't know, wouldn't he be safer with you?" she asks, trying to find any reason she can to let have to have that damned toad stool near her.

"Don't be ridiculous, of course he will be fine here with you. I will just leave him on the bed."

"Fine, fine. I will watch him for you."

Gerald lays Fergus down on the bed and puts his hood on.

"I expect to be compensated in some way for this." He retorts.

"I'm watching Fergus for you?" she replies with a raised eyebrow.

"That doesn't nearly cover it." He responds before ducking out of the room and leaving her alone in the quiet. Well, *technically* alone.

She scowls at the mould covered toad stool and curls up on the end of the bed, as far away from the toadstool as she can. She wraps her arms around herself and allows every moment of pressure, fear, and uncertainty to flood out in hot tears and chest aching cries.

CHAPTER TEN

The knock at the door startles Aedlin awake. She sits up in a panic and pulls her blade out. She places it discreetly beside her and hovers her hand over it.

"Who is it?" She calls out, trying to keep her voice from wavering.

"It's Olive." The voice from the other side of the door responds.

Aedlin relaxes her shoulders and places her blade back in her pocket. Her stomach grumbles, reminding her of the soup Olive had said she would bring up.

"Come in." She says as she wipes away the sleep from her eyes. She must have been out for longer than she expected. Her head feels all groggy and her muscles have a dull ache all over.

Olive comes in, empty-handed, and immediately Aedlin is back on high alert. Another set of footsteps comes from behind Olive, somewhere behind her, and Olive gives Aedlin a look of caution. She once again reaches for her blade; Olive shakes her head at Aedlin as if to tell her not to, but Aedlin pays her no attention.

"Aedlin, I would like to introduce you to someone. Can you please get to your feet?"

"Who?" she demands, staying in place.

"King Ulrich Mymar of Khard. Rather than sending his men to retrieve you, he has travelled personally to ensure your safety during your travels to his castle."

Aedlin gets up but keeps herself at the ready. No amount of being told just how nice he is will make her actually believe it.

Olive steps to the side and a large man with hazel eyes and a black, sculpted stubble enters through the doorway. He looks rough around the edges, aged beyond his actual years. His thin, long black hair sits snug behind the hood of his stained cloak. The only signs that he isn't some homeless man she has found off the street are his well-manicured fingernails and almost perfectly white teeth; and of course, the lack of thick booze scent, in fact he smelled over powerfully strong of lavender.

"Could you give us a moment please, Olive?" He says with a smile that makes the wrinkles around his eyes deeper.

"Yes, of course." She replies, noticeably pushing her chest out further towards him and Aedlin rolls her eyes.

"I'm sure you have every reason in the world not to trust me. I understand. I wouldn't trust me either." He begins, Aedlin accidentally scoffs at his more than obvious statement, but he appears to choose to ignore it.

"I wish to be able to assure you than I mean you no harm in any way, but I expect that I would be right in assuming you are far too smart to have your walls down around anyone, let alone anyone new, let alone again, someone in power."

He pauses and stares expectantly at Aedlin.

"Go on." She insists, curious to know what he has to say.

"I have given it some thought. I believe there is only one way I can gain your trust in a timely matter, because, after all, time is something neither of us seems to have much of."

Aedlin relaxes the muscles on her back but keeps her hand that is still hovering over her blade.

"How exactly do you think you can gain my trust?" she asks with a raised eyebrow.

"Because we have someone in common, someone who trusts me to keep the biggest, but most common, secret you can have across all of Agoura."

Aedlin's mind races to think of everyone she has crossed paths with since she left Malheim, after all, it's not possible he knows anyone from there... unless...

"Tell me who." She demands sharply.

"Seiche."

One word, one single word, is enough to shatter all the courage, strength, and power she thought she had.

"Do you know if she's alright?"

"Seiche? Yes, of course she is. She made sure to contact me to let me know she has relocated but won't tell me where to yet."

"Can you prove it?"

He rolls his shoulders back and looks past Aedlin. He stays like this long enough for Aedlin to become concerned.

"It will be difficult, but yes, I can." He finally says.

Aedlin begins to say something, but he interrupts her.

"But I can't do it here. The only way I can prove anything to you about Seiche being alive and to put your mind at ease is at my castle."

Aedlin raises a suspicious eyebrow. But to both her own and his surprise, she agrees to go with him.

"But before I go anywhere, I need Saviel and Gerald both located. The only reason they aren't with me now is because of something I did."

"I might be a King who is known for having love and compassion for all who reside in my kingdom, but that doesn't mean I know the names of them all, I'm afraid I have no knowledge of who you are talking about."

"So, you won't help?" she asks quietly.

"That's not what I said. I just need you to tell me more about them so I can get my people out and looking for them."

Aedlin allows the relieved smile she can't help but make to stay in place. But it only lasts a few short seconds before another sobering realisation sets in.

"Will you allow for the both of them to stay in the castle too?"

He appears to mull over the question, rubbing his finger against his chin.

"Of course, whatever it takes to get you to come back to the castle with me, where I know you are safe."

"And can you ensure that neither of them knows that I am the one who is looking for them?"

His eyes widen, but he quickly corrects himself.

"Of course." His voice is weary, but Aedlin is glad he doesn't force a reason from her.

CHAPTER ELEVEN

Aedlin hadn't expected much beyond being offered one of the castles, she assumed, *many* guest bedrooms. Perhaps there would be a washroom she could use but would likely have to share with others in the castle, she thought perhaps, while on the journey to the castle from the bar that she might be offered some food, she would consider herself lucky if whatever that food was either fresh *or* warm, she allowed herself to dare hope for both. The King didn't say much of anything during the short twenty-minute carriage ride through Khard. Aedlin appreciated the lack of small talk, although she had let her mind wonder what would happen once she arrived at the castle. She spent the entire ride looking out of the small window of the carriage into the night, hoping to spot either Saviel or Gerald herself.

"Is there anything I can get you, miss?" A human woman with dark eyes, light freckles and bold red lips asks.

Aedlin startles at the sound of her, not noticing that she has passed her in the doorway.

"Miss?" The woman tries again while very casually wiping her hands over her white apron.

"Is there any chance I could have something to eat, please?" her cheeks were warm, she's not really sure why. She considers that perhaps it's more of a feeling of being out of place in someone else's castle, rather than just embarrassment.

"Of course you can!" she exclaims and rubs Aedlin's right arm. "There's no sense it lettin' those cheeks get all hot with shame over a request like that, darlin'. In fact, the King has invited you to join him for dinner, if you feel up to it, of course. If not, your dinner can be sent up 'ere to your room. Either way, it's a hot roast dinner, cow, I'm fairy sure, with all the fixings on the side, and it'll be berry pie and ice-cream for after."

Saliva fills Aedlin's mouth and her stomach growls

loud enough for the both of them to hear.

"I think I will join him; it seems the most well-mannered thing to do, especially after all of this." Aedlin waves her hand out, motioning to the room that is bigger than the one she had at home, she could see from the doorway that just like her own it had a bedroom, living area and bathroom but every one of those rooms were almost double what she had. Even the bed appeared to be almost double that of what she had, and the feather filled bedding looked comfortable enough to hide away for an entire winter in.

"Very well, miss. I will let him know." She bows her head a little and begins to walk away. Aedlin's eyes catch the doorway of the bathroom, and the temptation is too hard to fight.

"When will he expect me for dinner?" Aedlin asks.

"I would say not for another thirty minutes at least miss, why?"

"I was thinking of taking a hot bath beforehand."

The woman gives Aedlin a warm smile, and she rushes toward a closet that sits against the wall of the bedroom.

"That's no problem at all, miss. I expect you would like some fresh clothes to change into when you're done?" she looks down at Aedlin's dirt, mud and sweat stained clothes and gives her a questioning look.

Embarrassed again, not just because of the woman staring at her clothes now, but of the fact that she looked just like this while talking with the king.

"I don't have anything else on me and I've been travelling some distance now." Aedlin starts, feeling the need to tell her that there is a reason she looks the way she does.

"No need to explain yourself to me to miss, and you needn't worry yourself about your clothes. Lucky for you, almost everything in here should fit you nicely, or at least close enough to it. Pick whatever you like while I run you that bath."

"Are you sure I'm aloud?" Aedlin asks, sceptical that she would have access to someone else's clothes without either their direct say so or very likely some rather negative repercussions.

"Yes, of course. These clothes belong to the king's sister. She left years ago in search of a more exciting, adventurous life. Her heart was never for the crown, it was always travelling, even when she was just a child. So, the moment she could, she got on a boat and sailed away to explore lands beyond our shores without ever looking back."

The woman's eyes twinkle as she talks. Aedlin wonders if the woman was anything like Melody is to her and it sends an instant wave of sadness over her.

"And he kept her room as it was?" Aedlin asks, trying to distract herself by keeping the subject on someone else.

"It's a promise his late parents made him keep, one that he was more than happy to keep. They wanted her to always have her home to come back to, no matter how many years separate them."

Aedlin walks over to the clothes that are hanging in the closet and almost cries at the sight. The gowns that hang from the hangers are beautiful, each one's design featuring either intricate lace, beading or both. They are all slimmer-fitting and each one is floor length. From what Aedlin can tell, the lady was right. They should fit fairly well or close enough to it. She reaches out to trace her fingertips over the lace of a dark blue gown.

"Are you really sure this is okay?" she asks, unable to shake the feeling that she could be making someone extremely happy wearing such wonderful pieces.

"I promise you; it is perfectly fine, the King made the suggestion himself, he wanted your stay here to be comfortable, in order to do that he is offering you his sister's room and clothes. Please accept his offer."

Aedlin moves on to the next gown in line, a long-sleeved black evening gown with sparkles that shine like stars against the black backdrop and silver beading running along the deep neckline.

"Okay." she finally whispers.

The woman gives her a nod and hurries off into the bathroom. Quickly after the sound of running water fills the quiet.

She takes the time while waiting for her bath to familiarise herself with the bedroom more and the adjoining living room. She is used to having someone else do almost all tasks she has needed done, big or small and she had always felt somewhat odd about it, but at least that was in her own home, with fae she knew, with fae that watched her grow, who helped her grow. But here, in someone else's home, in someone else's bedroom, having someone tend to her needs feels more awkward.

She moves on into the living area. There is a small round wooden table positioned near the window with only a single chair sat with it. Just like her own living area, there is a lounge seat positioned in front of a currently unlit fireplace. But unlike her bedroom, there are bookshelves lining the entire left of the wall with no spaces to spare for even a single other book to be added. She rushes over and takes in the beautiful sight, allowing the excitement that is bubbling up inside of her to spill out into a joy-filled giggle.

"It sure is somethin' isn't it, miss?" the woman says from the bathroom door.

"It's beautiful." Aedlin responds excitedly.

"It's part of the reason that girl couldn't resist the pull of adventure. Going on adventures through the eyes of the characters in those books was never going to be enough for her." She smiles fondly and shakes her head. "Your bath is ready miss, just drop your clothes outside of the door whenever you're ready and I will get them all cleaned up and back to you by tomorrow afternoon."

"Actually, could I please get your help to get out of this darn thing?" Aedlin asks quietly.

"Yes, miss, of course." She says and hurries over to help. She makes quick work of the dress before stepping back and allowing Aedlin space to remove the dress.

"Thank you." Aedlin says as she passes the dress to the woman and heads straight for what she hopes will be the greatest bath she has ever had.

* * * *

"Right through these doors, miss. The King is waiting." The woman says, pushing open one of the wooden double doors in front of them.

"Thank you." Aedlin says and runs her hands over the skirt of the blue dress she chose from the closet.

"Oh, my goodness!" Aedlin exclaims, shocked at herself.

"What's wrong, miss?"

Aedlin places her hand on the woman's shoulder. "I'm so sorry, I haven't even asked you your name."

The woman places her hand over Aedlin's. "Oh miss, don't worry yourself about it, I'm sure you have more than enough on your plate, I never even noticed."

Aedlin worries that the woman is just trying to be kind, but her warm smile seems genuine.

"Please, tell me your name." Aedlin insists.

"It's Livanna miss."

"What an absolutely beautiful name."

"Thank you, miss." Rivanna says as her cheeks are pink.

"Please, call me Aedlin."

"Oh no miss, I couldn't."

"I insist." Aedlin says, lowering her hand from

Livanna's shoulder.

"Very well, Aedlin, now you best get in there. The King is a wonderful man, but no one likes to be kept waiting when they're hungry." She gives Aedlin a wink and it makes her giggle.

She enters the excessively sized dining room where King Ulrich is waiting at the end of a dining table that spans almost the length of the while room. King Ulrich says something to her, but she hardly notices. She is too taken aback by the table. Rather than being a usual basic shape, instead the table has been left as the shape of the tree was when it was cut. It's a beautiful idea that she is in love with.

"Aedlin?" King Ulrich says, trying to get her attention.

"I… I'm sorry." She stammers and takes a seat at the only place where a second place setting has been positioned.

"Your table is beautiful." She says as she squares her shoulders and prepares herself to take on any questions the King is guaranteed to have.

"Thank you, I have many loved possessions, some worth more than I'm comfortable admitting out loud, yet this table sits high up in the list of one of my favourites."

Aedlin chooses not to respond, she doesn't want to

risk temptation by asking what other possessions he has and give away that she most likely knows herself how much at least some of them are worth, or, also likely, that he owns something crafted by fae-kind some time ago, before they were locked away for survival.

"I see you've changed out of your disguise." She quips.

"I see you have to." He responds with a raised eyebrow.

Her heart sinks at the realisation that she was right and he's obviously not happy about her wearing his sister's clothes. But then, as his words echo in her ears, her breath hitches. She does her best to play off what he said.

"Livanna told me what is being served for dinner. It sounds wonderful. In fact, your hospitality since I stepped into your home has been beyond wonderful, and I am very grateful."

"Although one of us is still keeping part of our disguise, isn't that right? Aedlin, princess, no sorry, queen of Malheim."

Aedlin's mind is in overdrive, she needs to get out of here, she should have trusted her initial instincts, no amount of good deeds and will towards the people in his kingdom is enough to prove that you can trust someone in his position, she had been taught that so early on and yet, the first time she is put in a position where she needs to put her teachings into practice she gets everything wrong.

She considers the idea of making a run for it, but she doesn't know her way to the doors they entered through from here, not that leaving through there would be any use, they came in from the main entrance which is over-flowing with guards and staff, and she certainly hadn't bothered to notice any other exits.

"Aedlin please, breath."

Breath? He just revealed to her that he knows who she is! How could he expect her to be calm? Does he know there is more than just her? He has to, of course he knows of seiche! But what about beyond that? Does he know where Malheim is? Does he know that it is rich with fae and the magic that has been banned outside of it? Does he know that Malheim is home to the elder tree?

"Aedlin, I only told you that I know who you are, so you will know that you can trust me."

"How does that prove that you can be trusted? How is it possible that you know who I am?" she gets up from the table and backs herself away from him. She expects him to get up and try to stop her, but he stays in place.

"I know who you are because Seiche trusted me

enough to tell me, in fact, she trusted me enough to promise her that I would care for you and that when the time is right, I would help you return home to your people who will be awaiting your arrival, when the time is right."

"You know about the fae in Malheim?" she whispers, backing up more.

"Of course I do. Seiche discovered that someone from within Malheim was betraying your mother and had opened communication and trade lines with others. It was rumoured that his plan was always to overthrow you once the time came for you to take your place as queen."

Aedlin remains silent, there is no way for him to know so much without knowing someone who was directly connected to Malheim, Aedlin hadn't known it at the time, but Melody had made it clear that Seiche was very much part of the kingdom even though she had left.

"Seiche told you all of this?"

"Yes."

Some doors open to the side of the room and an elf pushes in a carriage covered with food and proceeds to lay it out on the table, another elf enters, a female this time with another cart, this one carrying a few different selections of wine and glasses, she wordlessly joins the male elf in setting out the table.

"Thank you Malfyre and Sylnee, please, make sure the both of you eat before you clean the kitchen."

The both of them thank him quickly before leaving back out of the same side door they entered through and close it behind them.

"Why?" Aedlin asks.

"Why what?" The King responds while beginning to dish up food onto his plate with a smile.

"Why would Seiche tell you all of this? It's not your business to know."

"It certainly is when your mother had arranged for my kingdom to be a safe haven for you, even before you were born. She arranged it with my parents, not me, of course. And they had mentioned something about you a few times over the years, but never who you really were or why I wound need to offer you haven. I got all of that from Seiche because she was there with your mother when she arranged it all with my parents."

He looks over the bottles of wine before settling on one and pouring himself a glass.

"Please, join me, eat something while we talk. I do hope you won't think I am being rude, but you could do with a decent meal."

Aedlin looks over the table full of food. It was already

getting difficult enough to resist the smell, but the sight of it made it near impossible. Roast beef, roast vegetables, fresh, crisp salad, fresh baked bread. Her mouth fills with saliva and she caves.

She sits back down and immediately begins filling her plate, ignoring the fact that she's very aware that King Ulrich can see how much she is piling on. He grabs a glass and pours more wine before placing it down for her.

"Thank you." She mumbles and immediately picks it up and downs the entire thing.

Without saying a word, he pours her another.

She shovels the food into her mouth, ignoring how hot it all is and how multiple places on her tongue are burning. She knows that everything she eats and drinks for the next week now is going to taste bland and her tongue will probably annoy her to the point that it will become maddening but right now neither her, nor her stomach care very much about that at all.

King Ulrich lets her continue to eat in peace until her plate is almost half empty and she has finally slowed down.

"I hope you find your room comfortable, you should be able to manage a good night's sleep in that bed, and if it will make you feel better knowing it, I plan on having a few of my guards on rotation at your door for the duration of your stay, to ensure your safety."

She's has grown too suspicious of him, even after everything he has told her to be able to trust that the guards will be for her safety and not to ensure she doesn't leave the room throughout the night, but for now, she chooses to let it go.

He places his knife and fork down, takes a sip of wine, and clears his throat.

"I have something I need to ask you about. If that's alright with you, of course?"

Aedlin suddenly loses her massive appetite. She doesn't know how much more she can take. At least she knows she doesn't have many secrets left that she has to keep from him, she supposes.

"What is it?"

"I had been told that it appears you were a rare exception of a fae who was born without any magical abilities, and yet, I'm told you did something quite extraordinary at the bar, well, extraordinary for a non-magic using folk."

Aedlin looks down at her hands, turning them over and back again, looking at them as if they were no longer familiar to her. She had barely allowed herself a moment to dwell on or question what had happened, so she isn't exactly sure what she is able to tell him.

"What's your question?" she finally asks, realising he is waiting for her to say something.

"Was that you, or someone else? I only ask because I need to know so I can ensure the protection of whoever else it was."

She lets her shoulders relax; the question is simple enough to answer compared what she had expected.

"It was me."

"Very good. Well, your protection as a magic user is already under way, so I guess we can check that off."

Aedlin picks her fork back up but just pushes a carrot around on her plate.

"If you're finished eating, you are welcome to familiarise yourself with your new temporary home, or just go to your room for the night if you want to rest. I know it's been a bit of a day."

The offer to rest it tempting, but how can she when she knows Saviel is still probably out somewhere disgusted by her and Gerald is probably still looking for him?

"I don't suppose you've heard anything about the whereabouts of Saviel or Gerald?" his mouth twists into a frown and she takes a sip from her wine.

"I'm sorry, I assure you, as soon as they are located you will be informed, and we will arrange for them to be bought here."

"Perhaps I could go help look for them? The only reason they need to be found in the first place is because if me." She says softly as she plays with a stay pea on her plate.

"I know you want them found, but you are no good to anyone out there, risking your life, not when you have a kingdom waiting for your return. I have some of my best men out there looking for them. They won't return until both of your friends have been found."

Aedlin sighs. As much as she wants to argue with him, she knows he is right. She wants nothing more than to return to Malheim where she belongs and in order to ensure she gets there; she needs to keep herself alive.

"Speaking of my return to Malheim, when exactly am I able to return?"

This time it is his turn to take a drink from his wine.

"How long ago did you leave?"

"Around three days, maybe four, they started to blend together a bit. Why?"

"It's been longer than I thought. I certainly don't blame you for feeling restless and wanting to return home. Especially for someone who has never been away from it before."

"How long Ulrich?" she repeats angrily.

"Not until Seiche contacts me again to inform me that those who invaded have left."

"They're still there?" she shouts.

"Last I heard, yes."

Aedlin's heart sinks deep into her chest. It pounds loud enough to hear it in her ears and her breathing grows more rapid by the second. She can feel a panic attack coming on, and the last thing she wants is to have it in front of King Ulrich. She knows she can't return to Malheim yet but the desire to steal the horses and carriage she was bout to the castle in is almost too strong for her to push down, so she decided the best thing for her to do right now is hidden away in the room she was given and come up with a plan for sunrise.

"Actually, I think I might just call it in for the night. Please make sure I am woken up if Saviel or Gerald have been found."

He begins getting up from the table, but Aedlin shakes her head and gets up herself.

"Please, just promise me I will be told."

"Of course."

"Goodnight, King Ulrich, and thank you for everything. Dinner, letting me stay here, letting me borrow your sisters' clothes and, of course, keeping a promise to my mother."

"Of course." He says politely, but there is definitely some scepticism within his words.

Aedlin takes one last drink to finish her wine and heads for the door. She barely gets a chance to open it when King Ulrich calls her name.

"Yes?" she asks, turning.

"I am very sorry for the loss of your mother. I obviously never met her but my parents highly of her, on the rare occasions that they did speak of her. I know how it feels to lose your parents. I know it's no consolation, but I want you to know you're not alone."

Aedlin gives King Ulrich one last flat smile. She doesn't think she has it in her to muster up any more energy to accidentally be trapped into a conversation. She hurries out of the door so fast she doesn't notice the guard standing on the other side and bumps right into him.

"I'm so sorry." She mutters and runs her hands over his chest to straighten out his clothes.

"It's perfectly fine miss. He says and steps back away from her.

She realises she was likely making him uncomfortable by trying to fix his clothes.

"I'm sorry." She repeats and quickly turns away to leave but it doesn't take her long to realise that she had spent way too much of her time chatting with Livanna and not enough time familiarizing herself with her surroundings.

"Let me show you to your room, miss." The same guard she bumped into says as he comes up behind her.

"Are you sure you're allowed to?" she asks while looking toward the doors she just came out of.

"Of course, I'm allowed, miss."

Part of her wants to find a reason to protest. She could do with the time alone, but what would that accomplish? She would be left to wonder around the castle aimlessly until she eventually manages to find her room and she was far too tired for that tonight. It does, however, sound like a good plan for early morning. There has to be a reason for her mother and Seiche to have trusted the king's parents and, in turn- him. She will need to do whatever it takes to find out as much as she can. And starting as early as possible with a rested mind sounds like the perfect way to accomplish that.

"Thank you, I'd appreciate that." Aedlin finally responds.

He politely nods and informs the other guard who had been standing with him that he will be right back, the other guard responds only by nodding but that seems to be enough of a response for the guard who is helping Aedlin.

"I can check with the King to see if we can assign someone to escort you around the castle, just until you have grown familiar enough yourself."

Aedlin looks up at the guard and accidentally stops following him. Can she say no to him? She's sure it would come off as suspicious if she did, which means tomorrow's plans are ruined, but if she agrees, her plans are ruined either way. She hesitates but decides to try her luck by rejecting his suggestion.

"No that's okay, I'm sure I will find my way around soon enough, thank you for your offer to help though."

The guard continues walking up a flight of stairs. "No problem miss, please feel free to let any of the guards or other staff know if you change your mind."

"I will." She mumbles, trying her best to hide her surprise that he didn't protest or insist.

They continue in silence up the staircase until they reach the top where they turn right, continue down that hall until the end, enter through another door then turn right, into a hallway that finally looks familiar.

"Second door on the right, miss." The guard says before giving her a nod and leaving her.

"Second on the right... the one with a guard in front of it. Just like the King had said he would." She mumbles to herself but at this point she is both too tired to care and honestly a small part of her is relieved that someone will be outside, making her feel as secure as she would if she was in her own room in her own home, well, almost as safe.

"Miss." the guard at the door says with a nod as she closes the gap between them.

She nods back and he steps out of her way to allow her into the room.

She enters the room that doesn't belong to her and closes the door behind her before letting out the breath she didn't know she had been holding.

"The toadstool!" she exclaims, panicked while rushing to the bathroom to make sure it was still sitting beside the sink where she had left it when she went for her bath earlier.

Thankfully it is exactly where she had left it, but she decides she can't leave it here where it can be seen any of the staff who will no doubt come in to clean, she needs somewhere better than this where she can keep it safe until she can return it to Gerald who is no doubt worried sick about it.

She grabs a dry washcloth from the bench beside the bath and uses it to pick up and then wrap the toadstool in.

She considers hiding it in the closet until she can return it to Gerald but quickly decides against it, there is definitely a smell emanating from the toadstool and she would hate to ruin the clothes that are in the closet by allowing that smell to bleed into them.

She frantically looks around the room, wanting to just hurry up and find somewhere so she can go to bed. Before she gets a chance to find somewhere, there is a knock at the door and Livanna calls out her name.

Panicked, she decides to put the toadstool in the drawer of the bedside table and calls out for Livanna to come in.

The door opens and Livanna enters with a small plate with a piece of berry pie on it and a pitcher of ice water on the other. As well as balancing a drinking glass under her arm. Aedlin rushes over and takes the pitcher from her hand.

"You didn't need to carry these all the way up here." Aedlin says and places the water down on the little round table.

"It's no trouble, miss." She says and places the pie

down by the water. "I've also come to show you where you can find clothes to sleep." She continues.

"Oh, I hadn't even considered it. I'm so tired I could happily plop down on the bed as I am now and sleep for a week." Aedlin giggles.

"Well now, we can't have that, follow me into the living area and I will show you where you will find something to sleep in."

Livanna leads Aedlin into the living and to a closet matching the one in the bedroom that she hadn't noticed earlier when the books had her full attention. Livanna opens the closet for Aedlin then steps back, allowing Aedlin to take a look.

"Just like other the clothes, you are welcome to whatever you'd like."

"Thank you, Livanna, this all still feels very strange, it's one thing to use an expression like walking in another shoes, but to literally do it is making me feel very out of place."

"Please don't let it trouble you miss, the princess would be delighted that she was helping someone in need, especially if all it took was to share her room and clothes." Livanna removes a stray hair from the shoulder of the dress Aedlin is wearing, it's a small, probably very casual gesture to her, but Aedlin's heart swells at how much Livanna reminds her of Melody.

"Thank you again." Aedlin says quietly.

"You a very welcome, miss. It's time for me to retire to my room for the night. If there is anything you need, please ask the guard who is standing by your door. He will take care of whatever or whoever you need."

Aedlin doesn't respond. She just gives Livanna a tired nod and waits for her to leave before deciding on a simple white cotton nightdress.

She changes quickly and forces herself to stay awake long enough to wash her face and clean her teeth before finally curling up under the bed and letting herself sink into the mattress, succumbing to her exhaustion.

CHAPTER TWELVE

Saviel drops to his knees in the dirt. The cold of the late-night air is nothing compared to the ice that fuels his guilt and hatred for the home that sits abandoned and crumbling, succumbing two nature's elements. He can barely make out the front door that is half fallen off its hinges, the broken glass from the one of only three small windows that surround the house.

For the briefest of moments, it felt as though the ice that surrounded his heart for so many years might have been beginning to melt. It sounded so cliché and he hated that. Falling for someone isn't something Saviel had high up on his priority list, or even at all. It's not something he deserves for himself, because of him, his mother and father, two people who were more in love than anyone he had ever known, never got the chance to live the full life they deserved. His mother had told him that their love was formed under a starless night, but the moon seemed so close they could almost reach out and touch it and that Saviel and his brother had been born children of the winter sun.

No, he can't think of him right now, it's one thing to let the ugliness of his guilt over his parents' death bare its foul teeth but he cannot allow himself to feel the pain of remembering what his selfishness did to Oriis.

With trembling legs, he forces himself to get to his feet. He should never have come back here, he has managed to stay away since that night, he has returned to Khard countless times now, always managing to resist temptation and it was always easy to leave and get back on the road in the complete opposite direction his nightmare.

It's just not as easy as that this time, now that he knows who Aedlin *really* is not only should he not give a damn whether she is still sitting up in that room or not, he should not care that he has left her completely vulnerable to that group of drunks who made it clear she had something they wanted and are no doubt pissed because they don't have it, not to mention she dropped the lot of them on their arses which Saviel is sure is worse than actually physically hurting them they? would have taken a pretty big blow to their ego, which for some, is enough to send them off the rails.

He should top up on supplies and do what he has always done when it starts to feel like he has been back for just a little too long-get the hell back out, but he can't shake her. Aedlin's words ring between his ears, pleading with him to remember the version of her he had gotten to know over the last few days and to his dismay that's exactly what almost every fibre in him wants to do, it's very quickly winning against the part of him who wants go to the outer lands surrounding Khard's few remaining farmlands, find one of the dark elf king's guards and inform them of what he saw her do. They would be very interested to know that not only are there still fae around but at the very least one of them has been breeding with a dark elf. He shudders at the thought, everything he grew up learning and being told about the two kingdoms certainly didn't include anyone *ever* falling in love with the other side.

He sighs, slumps his shoulder and begins the walk back to the tavern, he doesn't have to speak to Aedlin tonight, or even again at all, but he won't allow himself to do to her what he did to his family. He will return to her and ensure he is safe before he leaves Khard at early light.

* * * *

Saviel returns to the tavern. It's much quieter now. It's odd, even for this late hour. Olive has probably decided to close early for the night after what happened, Saviel considers. He also considers how pissed she's going to be about the loss of money she would have made for the night had he not bought Aedlin here, had he not opened his trouble making mouth and had he not been stupid enough to think he would ever be able to allow the chill within him to warm?

He shakes his head, feeling defeated and dog tired. He sets his plan in mere seconds. Check with Olive to make sure Aedlin is fine. Sleep, then leave before Aedlin wakes in the morning.

"There you are!" Gerald shouts from across the bar. The relief in his voice pulls Saviel's attention.

"What's happened?" Saviel asks, eyeing the king's guard that's standing by Gerald. His stomach drops at the sight of him. Something's happened to Aedlin. Those losers from earlier came back. They must have.

"Aedlin has been taken to stay with King Ulrich. He

has requested that, for our safety, we accept his invitation to stay with him, too." Gerald slides off the stool and collects his bag from the floor.

Stay with the king? For what? It makes sense. He supposes that he would want to take part in keeping Aedlin safe. But she is none of his concern, not anymore, and he is surprised that Gerald is so eager to go.

"You want to go?" Saviel asks, shocked that Gerald would agree to something like this so easily.

"Not particularly. I have a business to run and so far, I'm off to a slow start; not that I'm blaming you or her for that. But I'm a father first, and she has taken Fergus with her."

Saviel shakes his head disapprovingly. "Why does she have Fergus?"

"Because she begged me to go out looking for you, well, more like demanded. So, I asked her to watch Fergus while I did. The poor thing needs to rest after the day he's had."

Saviel stumbles back half a step as the warmth returns inside him just a little more.

"She wanted to find me?" he asks, needing to make sure he heard right.

"Yeah? Gerald asks with a raised eyebrow. "Why

should that surprise you? You can't tell me you haven't noticed how she looks at you, you should have seen how worried she was when you left."

"Fine, we accept your offer." Saviel says to the king's guard before he can once again over think things and no doubt change his mind. The guard, who had begun impatiently tapping his foot, stands to attention and with a nod and leads them back outside to a waiting carriage Saviel hadn't noticed on his way in.

CHAPTER THIRTEEN

Aedlin stirs. There is a banging somewhere in the distance, but at this moment, she couldn't possibly care less if she tried. She pulls the blanket up over her shoulder and relaxes back against the pillow. To her dismay, the banging continues. She opens her eyes long enough to see that it is still dark out. She cusses and sits up, deciding to get herself a glass of water. When she hears banging again before she even gets the chance to place her feet on the ground. This time the sound of it makes her startle at the realisation that the sound was coming from her door.

"Miss?" someone calls out just barely loud enough for her to hear. She gets to her feet and hurries to the door, cursing herself for not bothering to check for a robe in the closet when she picked out her night dress.

Aedlin opens the door to a different guard than who was standing watch when she returned earlier. Not that it was easy to tell right away, so far, every one of the guards she had encountered since arriving had almost the exact same broad shouldered, square jawed and masculine enough to know they a threat look. She did consider it interesting that they all, so far, are human.

"What is it? is something wrong?" Aedlin asks the waiting guard.

"No, nothing is wrong, miss. The King has requested that you to join him in the dining room."

"At this hour?" she asks, folding her arms over her chest in an attempt to stop the cool air coming in from the hallway from making her shiver. "What could he possibly need this late if nothing is wrong?" she continues.

"It's not my place to say miss, just please follow me. I will lead you to the dining room to ensure you don't lose your way."

Aedlin closes the door behind her and wraps her arms tighter around her chest as she follows the guard back to the dining hall.

When they arrive, the doors are already wide open, and she can hear Saviel and Gerard talking with the king. She drops her arms to her sides and sucks in a nervous but surprised breath through clenched teeth. she had hoped the King would manage to locate the both of them but didn't expect that he would be successful. she stops just before the doorway and out of their view. She's relieved to know that they're both okay but isn't sure how she is supposed to face Saviel, not after how they left the last time they saw each other.

"Miss?" the guard asks, his eyebrows narrowed. He looks just as worried as she feels, and she suspects it has something to do with how long it took her to wake up. The King seems fine so far but of course no staff likes to keep someone like him waiting. She knew that for herself, no matter how kind and patient she was with those who worked in her home, they were always in such a rush whenever anything had been asked of them by either her or her mother. Even a request from Melody would have them scurrying.

"I can't go in there." Aedlin whispers.

"But the King has asked that you do." The guard whispers back.

"I know and I don't wish to get you in any trouble, but perhaps you could request that he meet me out here or better yet up in my room?" she suggests.

"I don't want to step out of line, miss, but aren't you the one that requested that these gentlemen be found?"

"Yes, I was. I want them here so I can know that they're safe, but for reasons that are personal, now is not the time for me to see them."

"Aedlin, is that you out there? Gerald calls out from the dining room.

Aedlin's eyes widen in a panic. They flicker towards the staircase where she considers running back up them and going back to her room. The guard gives her a knowing look as if he can tell what her plan is and shakes his head slowly. His expression turns desperate, and she knows in that moment that she couldn't do that to him. Sometimes she hates that her conscience sits on her like this, but he's done nothing to deserve to be chewed out by the King and she won't be the reason for making that happen. Footsteps close the gap between them in the dining room and she takes a steadying breath to prepare herself for whatever is about to come when she and Saviel are once again face to face.

"Thank the gods you are alright!" Gerald exclaims.

"Of course she is. I told you she's safe here with me." The King says, rolling his eyes.

"I'd like to hear that from her so I can truly believe it." Gerald growls, to Aedlin's surprise.

"I promise you I'm fine Gerald, but what about you?" she asks?

"I'll be better once I have Fergus back. Where is he?" he reaches his hand out waiting for Aedlin to pass Fergus to him.

"Don't worry, he is safe, tucked away in one of the drawers in the room I'm sleeping in."

"You shoved him in some drawer?" Gerald asks, horrified.

Aedlin sees no point in lying about why she put him there. Perhaps it will help him see that carrying around a rotting toadstool is not healthy.

"Well, I did have him in the bathroom, but he was starting to stink the place out, so I wrapped him up and put him in the drawer. It was the only place I could think of to both keep him safe *and* keep the smell at Bay."

"You know, you're not as nice as you think you are."

"Can you please take him to my room so he can find Fergus? Aedlin asks the guard who had brought her down here. "Assuming that's alright with you?" Aedlin asks the king.

"Yes, of course." He mumbles, looking curiously at the two of them, as if he is trying to figure out what exactly it is they are talking about.

The guard leads Gerald away and up the stairs. The three of them remain in silence until the sound of their receding footsteps disappears entirely. finally, the King clears his throat. "I imagine the two of you have some things to go over. I'm sure this gentleman would like to know why you requested that he and the goblin be found and bought here." he doesn't give Aedlin a chance to protest, he motions for the only remaining nearby guard to follow him back into the dining room and he closes the door behind him.

Aedlin's mind races as she tries to figure out what to say that could possibly fix the situation. She had expected a negative reaction from him, but she hadn't expected that he would leave so suddenly without a word.

Saviel steps closer to her, and she braces herself for whatever is coming her way. She knows - well, at least she thinks she knows him well enough to know that he wouldn't do something to physically hurt her, but she also knows that he could say something to her that has the possibility of hurting just as badly. To her surprise, he continues to get closer to her silently, his eyes give nothing away about how he's feeling, once he's standing close enough to her that she could reach out and touch him which she wants with every fibre in her to do he stops. Her heart hammers heavy in her chest and she tightened her arms around her chest once again. This time, though, it's not to protect herself from the cold, let alone from whatever is about to happen. He reaches a hand out and places it over one of hers.

"Are you sure you're *really* okay?" he asks softly. "Now that it's just you and me, you can tell me the truth. If something is wrong, just say the word and I will help get the three of us out of here."

"I promise everything really is alright. I'm sorry I had the two of you dragged into this. I just needed to know you were both safe and the only way I could think to do that was to have you bought here. Now that I know you're safe and Gerald has Fergus back, you are both welcome to leave."

He doesn't respond he just removes his hand from hers and shakes off his cloak. He moves another step closer and drapes his cloak over her shoulders.

"Aedlin you're freezing."

She locks her eyes with his and her stomach flutters so hard she thinks she might be sick.

"Saviel, I mean it, once Gerald gets back down here the two of you should go. I know it's selfish of me but like I said I just needed to know you were safe and now that I know that I can accept that it's time for us to part ways just like we should have when we first arrived here."

"I couldn't leave even if I wanted." he says quickly

and shrugs.

"Why?" Aedlin asks. "What did the King say to you before I came down?"

She steps back suddenly worried about what she's about to hear She hadn't considered that obviously they had been having a conversation before her arrival.

Saviel doesn't answer and Aedlin presses further.

"Did he tell you that the both of you have to stay here?" Don't worry if he did. I did ask him to let you, but I won't allow for it if that's not what you want. You'll be out of here by morning at the latest just give me a chance to talk to him."

"He's not forcing us to do anything."

"Then why, I don't understand why you can't leave."

"I never said it was because I can't."

Saviel runs his hands through his hair and lets out a heavy sigh, he begins pacing, just a few steps back and forth in front of Aedlin. He stops for just a second and opens his mouth just a little like he is going to say something but quickly shakes his head and goes back to pacing instead.

Aedlin stops him by placing her hand against his chest. He lets out a low groan and places his hand over hers once again.

"Saviel please, tell me why you can't leave" he looks down at her, as their eyes meet, he tightens his grip on her hand and it sends an instant signal to her cheeks, reminding them that now is the time to pink up. She looks back up at him through her long eyelashes and gives him an embarrassed smile.

"Saviel." She presses once more for answers. His name leaves her lips as a barely audible whisper.

In one quick motion, he lets go of her hand, traces his fingers down her cheek, making her stomach clench. He continues down her face slowly until he reaches her chin. Pushes up on her chin and makes her head tilt back. Her lips part just a little in response and he uses the other hand to place at the small of her back, he pushes her closer to him and she gasps at the sudden movement, just as quickly his lips are on hers and in an instant she is lost in him, lost in the kiss, lost in the feel of his warmth against her the cold parts of her exposed skin and lost in the desperation and need coming through in the force of his kiss. He moves his hand from her chin to her hair and she moans appreciatively.

He kisses her harder in response, and she wraps her arms around his neck to encourage him to continue.

To her dismay, he pulls away. He takes a second to straighten himself up.

"This is. Why? I *won't* leave." He manages to say between breaths.

Aedlin had thought she was already dizzy from the lack of oxygen during the kiss, but that was nothing compared to now. Six words, six paltry words have completely shaken up everything in a matter of moments.

"What about back at the tavern? I know that showing you who I really am scared you off, does that suddenly not matter?" She asks trying to get a grip on the situation and figure out what this means for them.

Does she even want it to mean anything? She barely knows him, yet at the same time, besides her own mother and Melody, who have known her for her entire life, Saviel has learned more about her than anyone else in under a week. And she would be lying to herself if she didn't admit that she cared about him. She hadn't realised how much she really did care about him until he walked away. Even before, when she was nervous to see him, it was hard to deny the relief she felt knowing that he was safe.

"You matter more." Saviel whispers, interrupting her attempt to gather her thoughts.

And just like that, there's nothing left to put together. She knows she doesn't have the time to entertain forming something beyond what they already have; she knows that she has responsibilities beyond what she's ready to handle and she knows that there are still things that she has to keep from him to protect those that are relying on her but despite all of that; right here, right now, in this moment, she knows that she wants nothing more than to hear him tell her over and over again for the rest of forever, or at least as long as they get to have that *she matters more*.

Before either of them can say anything else, the dining-room door opens, and King Ulrich joins them once again.

"Do the two of you need more time? Or can it wait until morning? I'd had hoped to make it to my bed at some point this evening."

"Of course, it's late and we could all use some sleep." Aedlin says apologetically, although the King doesn't sound particularly annoyed, just tired.

"I'm sorry. I hadn't expected the two of you to be found tonight. I haven't organised anywhere for you to sleep. Just give me a moment and I will call someone down to turn over rooms for you." King Ulrich says.

"It's okay. I'd much rather stay close to Aedlin to ensure that she's safe. At least just for tonight." Saviel says and rests his arm along Aedlin's lower back and pulls her in close to his side.

"As long as that's alright with you." He quickly says, looking down at Aedlin.

He once again has her stumbling over her thoughts, he made it sound like both him and Gerald would be sleeping in her room, which would mean if he had any intention of discussing anything privately that just wouldn't be possible, besides there's only one bed in that room and although it's big she's not sure she's comfortable sharing it with the two of them or even just Saviel yet. Although it's hard to deny that she would feel much safer knowing that the both of them are close by rather than relying on the king's guards. She's sure the guards are probably perfectly trained and capable, but still, they're more strangers than Saviel and Gerald are, and she knows where she'd rather put her trust.

"That's alright with me, at least for tonight." Aedlin finally responds.

"That settles it then. I will send for someone to bring you fresh clothing and in the morning, you are all welcome to join me in the dining room for breakfast. We have much to discuss, and I always prefer to do it over a plate of good food."

Aedlin is immediately uneasy, not knowing what it is the King plans on discussing with them in the morning.

The King notices Aedlin's reaction and chuckles.

"Don't worry yourself over it, it's nothing you need to be concerned about."

She tries to find comfort in his reassurance, but until she knows for certain that she can trust him, she's going to have to keep her guard up. Hopefully, after she finds out whatever she can from whatever stop she can tomorrow, she will know if she truly can trust him, as everyone keeps trying to convince her.

"Shall we?" Saviel asks and gives her side to squeeze.

"Definitely, I'm exhausted." she responds and turns just in time to see the guard and Gerald returning from upstairs.

"Perfect timing." the King says to the guard as he approaches them.

"Please escort the three of them upstairs back to Aedlin's room."

"Of course." the guard responds and turns back around.

Gerald begins to protest but Saviel tells him it's just for the night and that seems to be enough for Gerald to follow them.

CHAPTER FOURTEEN

"Really, it's okay, the guard gave me enough spare blankets to make up a comfortable enough bed on the floor. I have slept in much worse conditions than this." Saviel shrugs. "Besides, I agree that it's not yet appropriate for us to share a bed and I would rather Gerald have the couch in the other room, so he feels like he has some privacy." He says as he lays two of the thicker blankets over the floor beside the bed.

"I will discuss better arrangements than this tomorrow morning with the king. If you insist on staying here, you should at least have a room with a bed to sleep in."

Aedlin says apologetically. She pulls the blankets up to her chest as she sits cross-legged on the bed and watches him make up his bed.

The gentle glow of a nearby lamp creates shadows that dance across Saviel. She watches them move as he does and loses herself for a moment in the mesmerising mix of light and dark. She considers sadly how much it seems to be a perfect representation of what the two of them have now gotten themselves into, she knows that for some reason, beyond the dark elves being terrible, that there is reason he reacted the way he did, being shocked about it she expected, but this was something different and now, as she looks at him and can feel the memory of the recent kiss still on her lips she can't help but feel that them trying to be anything, even friends is doomed from the beginning if they are going to pretend that she isn't who she really is and if they are going to continue to keep so much from each other.

She wants desperately for him to tell her why he ran from her, why he looked at her like she was a monster, but she couldn't allow him to expect the same honestly in return, could she?

"Saviel, tell me why you're running." The question is out before she can stop herself and she knows this is it, if he answers her she has to answer him in return and part of her is okay with that, part of her wants to share every detail of her life with him, about River and how she is like a second mother who she misses dearly, about her mother who she has not had the time to grieve and the truth about how she ended up on the cliff where they met.

"Why do I run? Or why I ran?" he asks, cautiously. She's not sure which one he would rather answer, but she knows she wants answers.

"Both."

He once again runs his hair through his hair and looks over towards the living area where Gerald is already laying on the sofa. Saviel says nothing for a few moments and a faint snore comes from where Gerald is sleeping.

Saviel relaxes his hands back by his side as soon as he hears the sound.

"May I sit?" he asks as motions toward the bed.

"Yes, of course Aedlin responds and moves over to make room for him next to her.

He takes a seat next to her and, for a long while, says nothing, just stares out towards something in front of him. Aedlin realises quickly that this was a mistake, and they should just go to sleep. If he wants to tell her anything, he will when he is ready.

"I'm sorry, you don't have to tell me anything."

"Yes, I do. I need to tell someone about this. I want to

tell *you*."

"You want to tell me why you ran from me?" she asks.

"Both." He says, repeating what Aedlin had said earlier. "They're sort of connected questions, he shrugs.

Aedlin adjusts the blanket back up under her chin and waits intently for Saviel to explain.

"I grew up on a farm. It belonged to my father's parents and when they could no longer keep up with the work, they sold it to my mother and father when they were newlyweds. Not too long after they had a handle on the farm thy had me and more years than expected later, they had my brother."

His voice begins to crack a little and Aedlin moves in closer to him. She hesitates at first but rests her head on his shoulder.

"I had realised at a pretty young age that growing and selling various vegetables was not something I aspired to do with the rest of my life." He shrugs. "For a while it fine. I could shove away the desire to find what else was waiting for me beyond the fence of our property. But eventually that desire became so strong I could barely take it, so, one day, my mother and father sat me down, they gave me permission to go out and find whatever it was my heart was looking for and handed me a sack with some essentials, a bottle for water, some vegetables from our farm and everything they had put away into savings over the years." His eyes lower and his lips tug into a slight frown. For a moment he doesn't say anything else and Aedlin decides not to press him further. But after a deep sigh, he continues. "At the time, I was too young and excited to see the size of the sacrifice they were making by both giving me their gold and losing the much needed an extra pair of hands they needed around the farm. That very same night, I did exactly as they had given me permission to do. I left to find more. I would be gone for weeks, sometimes months at a time, before I would return long enough to check in, enjoy some of my mother's cooking, and leave again."

Early on in my soul searching, I had begun hearing rumours that the dark elf King was trying to expand his kingdom and strangle the supply within Khard, and to do that, he was buying out farmers who surrounded Khard. If they didn't sell, he would kill them, the sick thing about it is he wouldn't even bother to keep the land of the ones he killed, it was no use to him if the farmers weren't going to continue to grow and harvest their crop.

The last time I left was the longest I had ever been away, there wasn't even a particular reason, I just got lost in the life of living it rough, meeting new folk, sometimes that included magic users, sometimes it included thieves. I think part of me stayed on the road so long this particular time because I was getting worried that my parents would ask me to come back and help them because I still hadn't found what I wanted."

He pauses for a moment, once again staring ahead, this time long enough to take a breath before continuing.

"Anyway, I finally decide I have left it far too long and make my way home, only when I return there was no home, just a busted down door, broken windows, upturned furniture, destroyed crops and the dead bodies of my mother, father and brother."

A burning lump forms in Aedlin's throat as tears balance on the edge of her eyes. He ran because he didn't see her, he saw the people who murdered his family. In an instant she is sick to her stomach, she slams her hand against her mouth, throws the covers off, stumbles out of the bed and sprints to the bathroom.

She drops to her knees and tries to suck in a deep breath. She knows her father is a murderer, but *his* family, and likely many others, did nothing. They just denied having their livelihood bought out from under them and for that they were killed, children were killed.

Aedlin Doesn't notice Saviel come into the bathroom until his hand is on her back.

"You don't need to be here." she protests.

"Of course, I do." he responds and rubs his other hand up and down the length of her back.

"Here." Saviel says as he passes her a glass of water.

"Do you feel well enough to get up?"

Her stomach continues to gurgle and she still feels like she can't breath so she decides it's best not to risk it.

"Not yet." she responds.

"Okay." He says and sits next to her.

She looks up, thanks him, and takes a small sip of the water. It does little suppress the feeling of wanting to throw up, but then again, how could it when the reason she wants to throw up is standing right in front of her? She doesn't know what to do or what to say, but she knows now that he deserves the truth more than ever. Even if it means risking losing him, but she's not selfish enough to keep him around, not when she knows what her father has done to him.

"Did you eat something bad at dinner, perhaps?" Saviel suggests as the reason why she might be sick.

"No, the food was fine." she whispers.

She places the glass down on the floor beside her, lowers her knees, and crosses her legs instead. She straightens her back and takes a breath. All the while unable to look at him.

"Saviel, I am so sorry for what happened to your family." she says as she nervously plays with her fingers.

"Thank you. I appreciate that, but you have nothing you need to be sorry for. King Erevin is a monster and so are all those who decide to join him. That is nothing for you to apologise for."

This is it; this is the last time she's going to get to see him, the last time she's going to be able to speak to him. Just barely an hour ago they shared their first kiss and now as she sits across from each other on the bathroom floor this will be the last they get to see each other because the truth will be too much for him to bare, it's too much for her to bare. how could she be expected to face him every day is a friend knowing that the monster who killed his family is her own family?

"Actually, it is something for me to apologise for." she whispers, barely able to get the words out.

"What are you talking about?" Saviel asks and worry lines quickly form around his eyes.

"The man who is the reason for parents' death even if he isn't the one who directly laid his hands on them, the dark elf king, is my father."

Saviel's mouth falls open and the hand had resting on her back is quickly pulled away. Aedlin waits for the inevitable to happen. For him to get up and leave like he did earlier, however this time she won't search for him, she will let him be, free of her and the darkness she carries with her.

"I don't understand." Saviel says.

Aedlin wasn't prepared for him to say anything to her and, because of that, find it hard to find the words to say.

"You're the lost daughter he's been looking for this whole time?" he says quietly.

"I had no idea he was looking for me until very recently, but yes, I suppose I am."

"So, the two of you have never even met before?"

"No?" Aedlin is taken aback by his questions. Why is he still sitting here with her? How is she still able to look at her without completely losing it, knowing who she is? Knowing what her father has done?

He reaches his hand back towards her and rests it on her knee.

"Then, as I said, you have nothing to apologise for."

Now it was Aedlin's turn to be confused. Of course she had something to apologise for. She had an entire country worth of people to apologise to for the unimaginable pain her father had bought upon so many lives.

"I don't understand." She says, repeating Saviel.

"As you said, you've never even met before. How could you possibly have anything to do with anything that vile man has done?"

Aedlin considers what Saviel is saying for a moment and for the briefest of seconds she lets herself consider that he is right. Until she is reminded that part of what her father has been doing is in search for her.

"People have lost their lives at his hand because of his search for me."

He moves his hand from her knee to her face where he rested against her cheek. She wants to lean into his hand and find comfort in his warmth, but it all feels so wrong now, the guilt is too heavy.

"Your father and his parents before him, and there's before them, have been slaughtering for the sake of growing their kingdom since long before you existed on it. yes lives have been lost in his search for you, and every one of them is a tragedy, but none of that is your fault, every one of those lives were lost because he chose for them to be, not you, this is not a guilt you need to be carrying, because it's not yours to bear."

Aedlin tries her best to hide the tears that begin streaming down her cheeks and her lip that begins to tremble.

Saviel attempts to wrap his arms around her, but she moves away. He ignores her rebuttal and tries again, this time pulling her into his lap and cradling her as she cries into his chest. They stay like this until her eyelids grow too heavy for her to be able to fight against it any longer.

She falls asleep to the feeling of Saviel carving his fingers through her hair as he sits silently, allowing her to release everything she'd been holding in since her mother's death.

CHAPTER FIFTEEN

Aedlin wakes just as the sun is beginning to break over the horizon. She checks to see if both Gerald and Saviel are asleep. As soon as she confirms that they are, she quietly checks the dresser for something to change into. She finds a black dress and boots to match. It's a little dressier than she had hoped, but she doesn't have time to be picky right now. Last night might not have gone as she expected, but her mind is clearer now than it ever was. She has a kingdom to return to, eventually, when it comes time for her to do that, but for now, it's time for her to meet her father. She hopes to speak with the King about her plan and slip away before Saviel or Gerard have any idea. She knows the both of them, particularly Saviel, would argue that is a bad idea, and the truth is she knows that it is. She knows that the likelihood of returning from her father's kingdom alive could be put down to wishful thinking. But she can't stand by knowing that he is killing people in search of her. She knows that there's been more death caused for far fewer reasons than this, but Saviel was wrong, she can't just let this not sit on her conscience and if that means having to tell the King that the very same man he's trying to do everything he can to protect his kingdom from is the father of the Princess he sworn to protect then so be it. With some luck he will help her on her way to find him, or he will probably banish her from his kingdom, either way she's one step closer to her father, and one step closer to putting an end to more lies being last in her name.

She slips out of the door and quickly asks the guard who was waiting outside of it to escort her to wherever the King is. Without hesitation the guard does exactly what she asks at leads her throughout the castle enter her surprise outside to the stables. there's the King is brushing down a large Black Horse. it's beautiful but she doesn't pay it much mind she doesn't have time to dwell on looking at the pretty horses as much as her younger self is hating her right now for not doing exactly that.

"Excuse me, King Ulrich?" Aedlin calls.

As soon as the King turns on shows that Aedlin has his attention that guard who escorted her here, leaves.

"I hadn't expected to see any of the three of you awake this early, you all seemed as though you could have used the rest."

She shrugs dismissively. "The others definitely need it, travelling can be rough and the both of them have done a lot of it. Thank you again for letting them stay here."

He places the brush back down into a bucket, gives a horse a final pat along its nose before stepping back and heading out of this stable.

"Are you coming? it's about time for breakfast." he calls after her but she stays in place.

Curiosity crosses his face as he turns back around to face her.

"Is something the matter?"

"I need your help; I need you to give me directions to my father."

He places his finger under his chin and rubs it. "I would be more than happy to help, except for a few problems with your request."

"What problems?"

The King walks back into the stable and positions himself much closer to Aedlin.

"Problems like I don't know who your father is and letting you leave to search for anyone, even your father, was not part of the promise that was made."

"Look, I'm grateful that you're doing what was asked of you by your parents and mine, but I wouldn't be asking if it wasn't important."

"And I wouldn't be telling you can't go if it wasn't important, Aedlin. its' not just about the promise that was made to keep you safe. It's about a promise that was made to keep everyone in your kingdom and mine safe, too."

She instinctively takes a step back. He still seems perfectly kind, but something about his nerves is putting her on edge.

"What are you talking about?"

"The promise wasn't just that I would keep you here and keep you safe, it was that once you had gained my trust enough, we would be wed and our kingdoms would be combined as a uniting force against King Erevin."

Aedlin's breath hitches and she once again steps back.

"That's not possible. My mother would never do something like that. She would never force marriage upon me, not even for the sake of our kingdom, or anyone else's is, for that matter."

The King frowns deeply and gives a sad look over towards the horse he had just been grooming.

"Listen, this is an arrangement I'm not particularly happy about either, but it's hard to pretend like this isn't a good idea. Our kingdoms were always going to be stronger together. If you need to see it, I have proof of this arrangement being made."

"I don't need to see anything; I know my mother would never have made this arrangement because she would never have expected me to singlehandedly have to go against the dark elf king."

"Don't sell yourself short. I'm sure she knew that you're stronger than you believe yourself to be. You would be surprised what you would do in order to protect those who rely on you most."

"I know she wouldn't do this because that would mean putting me against my own father."

Just as Saviel had the night before, the king's mouth falls open as he struggles to find the words to say.

"I don't have the time to give you my life story, but for right now, all you need to know is that I need to find my father to put an end to this madness. How can I be expected to hideaway in your kingdom when I could put an end to all this senseless killing by just giving myself over to him?" she shouts.

"And what exactly do you expect to happen when you arrive? do you think that suddenly because he's got his long-lost daughter back, he is going to stop killing? he will always find a reason, his type always do. Whether it be for land, to cleanse the world of magic using folk, or simply because he has decided that someone has done wrong by his thrown by denying him anything, ever."

Aedlin throws her head back, exasperated.

"I'm sorry to put an abrupt end to the life plan that had been laid out for the both of us, plans that I'm interested to know when you had originally planned to tell me about, by the way."

"Over breakfast this morning, I planned to tell you everything and to give both of your friends a place among my staff for the duration of their stay."

Aedlin rolls her eyes and shakes her head in disbelief.

"It's nice to know you had it all planned out." She retorts sarcastically.

The King slumps his shoulders in defeat. "I see no point in arguing with you. However, I will not send you to your likely death, especially when it would have been for nothing."

She wants to question what he means, but before she gets a chance, he calls out to some of his guards, who must have been waiting just outside.

"Organise a carriage. The two of you will be escorting Aedlin to Tarragor. I want her there by nightfall, so prepare to leave within the hour."

"So soon?" one of them asks.

"Yes, there is better to change of plans, but you will stick to your original instructions. You must take her there and ensure she makes it safely once she's there. The two of you are to return immediately."

"of course, right away."

"Miss, will you please follow us?" one of them asks Aedlin.

"Just give me a moment. I will meet you outside."

The same guard that had asked how to follow them gives a King a concerned look. The King nods and waves them away.

"There were plans to send me somewhere else? What happened to the plans for us to be married?"

"Yes, the plan was to have you sent to Tarragor. It's a secluded, small kingdom where every one of my guards is sent to train before they find themselves a place on my staff. I myself was sent there as a boy and my follow before me. In order to be the strongest we can be in our kingdoms, I thought it best for you to receive the same training."

"What does it matter now if I have no intentions of marrying you?"

"It matters so you can be prepared when the time does come for you to face your father. I can accept that I won't win this fight against you, but I won't let you go in unprepared. They know who you are, and they will take care of you just as much as I would. Just try to go in so hot headed, understand that not everyone in this world is out to get you and some of us do actually want to help."

Aedlin tries her best to convincingly agree to what he's saying, but honestly, how could he expect of her to not have trust issues? She only met him last night at every turn he seems to be popping up with no surprises.

"you'll need to leave now in order to make it before sundown. Would you like me to send someone for Gerald and Saviel?"

Aedlin accidentally gasps. She stepped closer to the King and narrows her eyebrows.

"No, you will not get them. You will not tell them where I'm going or why you will not tell them a thing about my father or that I came to you this morning asking for your help."

"They're going to notice that you're gone. What exactly do you suggest I tell them?"

"Just that I left and that they can stay here for as long

as the both of them need."

"Why would I let them stay here if you're not here? I have no need to protect them if I'm not needing to protect you."

Aedlin hates that she had a feeling he would do this exact thing to her, but she can't risk them trying to find her and putting their lives in danger because of her. she squares her shoulders and runs her hands over her dress to straighten it, she knows exactly what she can do to make him keep a promise as much as her heart hurts the idea, as much as she knows save, you'll won't understand her decision, she knows this is the only way to guarantee that the King will do as she asks of him.

"You will do this for me, you will keep them safe and you will keep some here, you will not allow them to follow me oh look for me and to thank you for that when I return I will marry you and help build a stronger kingdom for the both of us."

"I would agree that that sounds fantastic, but you can't guarantee me that you will return not if you're going to face your father."

"I suppose not, but just in case I do make it back, know that you have my word."

"Well, let's both hope that you do." He says dryly and once again calls out to his guards, who are waiting.

"Are you ready, miss?" One of them asks and this time Aedlin follows them across the grounds to an area where a number of carts are waiting, all with varying degrees of differences, some look much older and more common than others, like the one she rode in with the King last night. As she had suspected, she was directed to get in one of the older carts. She waits inside while the guards hook up two horses and gather basic supplies like water and some fresh fruit for the trip.

Very quickly, the two guards, who are now covering up their clothing with black cloaks, take their place outside of the carriage and immediately they begin they begin their departure of Khard.

She reaches down into the side of her loose-fitting boot and makes sure her blade is still secure before leaning back in the seat and closing her eyes, flashes of the kiss her and Saviel shared last night play over the darkness, followed by him cradling her on the bathroom floor as she cried into him, then flashes of Gerald and his stupid toadstool Fergus. She hadn't realised how fond of him she had grown too, even if he is incredibly annoying, and not exactly mentally sound. Part of her thinks it's sweet that he has founding something to love and care for as much as he does Fergus.

She opens her eyes and to her surprise they are already nearing the edge of thing kingdoms city limits. she looks out of the carriage window for a while, watching as they pass farms, some are rich with growth and others are left completely abandoned. In her heart she knows what that most likely means but she tries to allow herself the comfort of considering that perhaps they had just packed up and left in search for greater things, just as Saviel had.

She decides she can hardly take the sight of the homes any longer, part of her wants to force herself to look, to fuel the rage that has already built as a ferocious fire inside of her, she wants to greet her father for the first time with everything that he has done at the forefront of her mind, so when she does, whatever it is, she knows she has to do to finally put an end to this all, it will be in the name of everyone he has taken before their time.

But after they pass yet another abandoned home that has been trashed beyond repair she accepts that her heart simply can't bear it, not right now. So instead, she gives herself permission to close her eyes again, she gives herself permission to rest before she faces whatever is about to come next, and she gives herself permission to feeling the regret that sits with her for leaving the two men she wishes now she had of bought with her.

CHAPTER SIXTEEN

"We're almost Tarragor miss. It won't be too long before we reach king and Queen Valmir's castle." one of the guards calls from outside as they knock on the wall of the carriage.

Aedlin opens her eyes, sits back up, she looks outside, and notices is maybe only an hour or so before the sun begins to set. She rubs her eyes and tries to straighten out her hair; she hadn't expected at all that she would sleep for so long, but part of her is grateful for the peace and the rest before having to deal with whatever chaos she is about to walk into.

She grabs a drink of water and picks up a red apple. As she eats the apple in its entirety, she watches the kingdom come into view.

This kingdom is much smaller just as King Ulrich had described. She appreciates that at least something so far that has come out of his mouth has been honest.

She quickly finishes the apple and once again cheques for her blade and ensures that it's hidden from view. She hopes that she won't need to use it here, and it's likely she won't if there's any truth throughout the King had said about them being an ally and trustworthy, but it's not worth going in unprepared.

They pass a few farms, and pretty quickly they make their way through the heart of Tarragor. Unlike Khard, that is still reasonably busy in the late afternoon and night. Tarragor seems to be more of a sleepy town and, apart from the odd patron closing up for the night, she would have assumed it was a ghost town.

They continue on the same path until they reached the gates of a castle not much different from the size of her own. The small part of head tries to find comfort in that.

They stop at the gate weather gods talked to someone briefly before, however; they spoke to open the gate to let them through.

Aedlin Sucks in a deep breath through clenched teeth

and tries her best to ensure that whatever emotion she's got sitting on the edge right now is kept at bay. It certainly couldn't do any harm, she supposes, the King had asked if her and not go into this with a hot head.

The carriage stops at the bottom of a flight of concrete stairs leading up to the main entrance.

at the top of the stairs stands man and woman who are clasping each other's hands, there is a guard positioned on either side of them and as Aedlin watch is them she considers that it's the strangest thing that when one moves the other seems to be completely In Sync with them and in return so are the guards.

She shakes it off to an over imagination and maybe heightens nerves splashed with a little of paranoia. She gets out of the carriage in the last I cell phone moment, just stretches her legs out properly and straightens her dress.

"Wait here for just a moment while we explain who you are." One of the guards says.

"Why don't you go ahead? I think it would be best if I stay here with her just until we make sure that we are in the clear." The other guard says.

they gave each other a nod and the both of them watch is the guard climbs stairs and talks with the man and woman at the top.

the woman glances over the guard's shoulder a few times during their conversation and locks eyes with Aedlin.

At first, she is uneasy about the staring, but the woman gives her an apologetic smile or sympathetic she can't quite tell from so far away. Either way, for some reason, it brings her a great deal of comfort. Still, her guard will remain up, no dad until she leaves here and heads for wherever her father is.

The guard returns to them and gives the other guard a nod of confirmation.

"They were surprised that you are here early, as expected, but they are happy to take you in tonight and start your training first thing in the morning."

Aedlin thanks them both and, to her surprise, they immediately leaned back up into the carriage. She knows that the King had expected them back immediately after, but she hadn't expected that would have been so literal.

"Please come join us inside and get out of this cold." the woman says, even though she is practically shouting, her voice is still as soft as silk. Aedlin does as she says and meets them at the top of the stairs. To Aedlin's surprise, they don't exchange any pleasantries. Instead, they lead her straight inside. She follows them throughout the well-lit castle made of a combination of marble and stone until eventually they reach the kitchen. The mail tells the handful of staff were in there to leave until they were told to return and every one of them does just that without hesitation.

"Could we fix you a drink?" the woman asks.

Aedlin hesitates for a moment and resists the urge to lean down and reach for her blade. She's not quite sure what it is, but something doesn't feel right. The hair on the back of her neck stands on end and her mind repeatedly whispers for her to stay alert.

"Yes, thank you." She decides to respond, not wanting to arouse suspicion. She can certainly accept the offer, but she doesn't have to consume it.

Wordlessly the man crosses the kitchen, retrieves some wine glasses and a bottle of wine, then, with his back turned to Aedlin and the woman, he pours the wine. She tries to listen out for the sound of the wine pouring and, in case she manages to notice anything odd, perhaps a suspiciously long amount of time, where there isn't the sound of pouring. But she has no such luck because the woman begins making small talk.

"Is King Ulrich well? It has been so long since we last saw him. I had hoped he would have joined you on your travels here."

"Now Lulia, you can't expect the man to be able to leave his kingdom at the drop of a hat to make a sudden, unexpected delivery." The man says with a wink toward Aedlin as he carries two of the three glasses over.

Aedlin can't help but notice that only one of those two glasses contains white wine, the other looks to be more like water. The man passes Aedlin the wine and the other to his wife, she waits, watching intently to see if the woman will take a drink from her glass. She gives her husband a small peck on the cheek and thanks him before taking a sip.

The man goes to retrieve his glass of wine and when he joins the both of them again the wife raises her glass.

"To the hope of stronger kingdoms for the both of us, and to the soon-to-be bride and her wonderful-almost husband."

Aedlin's jaw drops, they know about the plans to marry and strengthen their kingdoms? Surely King Ulrich is a smarter than to believe that he could trust anyone else with that information. they would have had questions like who Aedlin is in where she came from. that would buy that she's just someone he came across and fell in love with. obviously, they would know that she has a kingdom of her own for how to bring to the table.

"He told you we plan to marry?"

"He told us there was a plan to marry not that you had settled on that plan, but we just figured seeing as you're here that plan is beginning to take shape."

Aedlin does her best to keep her tone flat.

"What else has he told you?"

"Really, he told us nothing about who you are, just that he would like to make sure that you received the exact same training as he had been gifted. He told us to consider at his wedding present to you, and well, I'm a sucker for love so it was hard to turn it down." the woman says with a smile and rests her head on her lower stomach.

Aedlin pause for a moment and takes in what's playing at in front of her, the Wiz now smiling down affectionately towards her stomach, and she looks to be drinking water instead of wine.

"You're expecting?" Aedlin accidentally blurts out.

"I am yes. We just discovered a few weeks ago."

"That's wonderful." Aedlin Mumbles, not sure what else to say. She glances once more at what appears to be a madly in love couple swooning over her pregnancy. King Radaven's eyes twinkle every time he glances down at his wife's stomach and Aedlin finds herself wondering if their baby will be more elf like its mother or human, like its father. She does know one thing for certain: this baby, although made from two different races, will never have to hide away who they really are, and the thought makes her smile. She makes the decision that the wine is probably fine, and hell, right now she could use an entire bottle of it. She pushes away the urge to down the whole glass, instead taking a polite sip. It appears to taste fine, and she decides to trust that it is. After all, how harmful could they really be? Perhaps she really had jumped the gun on this one and should have given King Ulrich the benefit of the doubt.

"To the expecting couple." Aedlin says, raising her glass. They join her in raising theirs before bringing them back down and taking another drink. This time Aedlin takes more of a mouthful and smiles a little as she watches the woman in front of her drink her water. she flicks her eyes over to the man who she's now realising hasn't lifted the glass to his lips once.

"What have you done?" she asks as the tips of her fingers begin to tremble and she loses grip on her glass. It crashes to the floor below, shattering at her feet. She begins feeling lightheaded and wobbly on her legs.

"I knew it, damn it, I knew it, I knew that there was something wrong." Aedlin says but it comes at as a squished together slur.

Her eyes try to shut as her eyelids grow heavier, but she fights to keep them open. The man approaches her side and wraps his arm around her waist to support her weight.

"Why?" she tries to ask, but it comes 's just a groan.

"You need to believe we really are so sorry for this. But it's the only way to ensure that there is a kingdom left for our child to be born into." the woman says with sadness about her face.

"Screw you!" Aedlin tries to shout, but the words are barely audible.

She feels her weight completely give out and realises with horror that she's relying completely on the men that's holding her up's left herself alone and vulnerable, like a stubborn fool.

"How much longer?" the woman asks. Her voice is shaky, as if she's nervous, but there is also sadness within it.

"Not long now, she won't be able to hold on for much longer." the man responds and shifts his grip on Aedlin to make it tighter.

Aedlin's breathing goes from panicked to shallow as she feels more and more of her body betraying her and succumbing to whatever it is that's flowing throughout her body.

Her knees buckle from under her as she continues to lose the fight.

"She's nearly gone." the man says a little too close to

her ear and fear ripples through her. The shaking in her hands gets worse, but this feels different, this feels familiar, recently familiar. She musters every tiny little of strength she has left in herself and cries out with everything she has as she slams her hand against the man. She opens her eyes just enough to see that he's now on the ground just as she had hoped.

"No!" the woman cries at but Aedlin ignores her, she knows she really has mere seconds to get this next bit right before she is completely gone. By some miracle she finds the strength to reach into her boot, retrieve her blade, and gives in to the feeling of her falling, she leans into it making sure to aim the blade anywhere she can on King Radaven. The last thing she sees before everything goes black is the blade passing through the middle of his thigh.

CHAPTER SEVENTEEN

"How mad do you think the King is gonna be that we stole a carriage and his horses?" Gerald asks from the seat beside Saviel.

Saviel can barely hear Gerald's question over the sound of the wind rushing past them as he directs the horses to continue on as fast as they can.

"I just ask because I'm already a tremendous disappointment to my family, you know, because of deciding to leave home and all. If they find me locked up by the king, they'll abandoned me."

Saviel shakes his head at the ridiculousness of Gerard's priorities. How can he care that he is risking prison knowing that Aedlin has decided to take off alone, to face her father?

He looks down at the goblin, who is stroking the top of Fergus slowly. He can't tell for sure, but it appears there is a tear rolling down Gerald's cheek and suddenly his frustrations are gone, mostly.

"Look, if the King didn't want us to go out and find her, he wouldn't have told us where he sent her. Let's just be glad that we know for sure that she definitely has not gone straight to find her father. At least the King was smart enough to ensure she had an escort."

"I suppose that's true." Gerald says with a shrug.

"Listen, right now we just need to get there and bring her back safe, and of course, talk some sense into her. After that, we can figure out the rest. If it does come to it, you have my word that I will not let you go to prison for this."

"You're a good elf." Gerald says and reaches up to pat Saviel on the shoulder.

The sound of it makes him feel that uneasy, but he pushes that aside and focuses once again on the task at hand, which is making these horses go as fast as they for as long as they can. All the while trying to not let himself think too much about what could be happening to Aedlin. Of course, she could be fine just as a King Ulrich kept trying to reassure them, but until he sees that for himself, he can't allow himself to believe it.

* * * *

They arrive at the gates of the castle just as the sun begins to break over the horizon.

Saviel is aware that he worked the horses far too hard, and for that he feels a tremendous guilt, but for right now he just relieved that they're finally at Tarragor.

"How do you suppose we get through the gate?" Gerald asks as they approach the castle.

"Well, I suppose it shouldn't be their problem if Aedlin is perfectly fine and really is here for the reasons that King Ulrich says she is."

"And if that's not the case?" Gerald asks with a raised eyebrow.

"Then I sincerely hope blood doesn't make you uncomfortable."

Gerald's eyes widened at Saviel's words, but he says nothing. Saviel watches as Gerald slips Fergus into his pocket ads it proceeds to give Saviel a nod to confirm that he is ready.

Saviel Ties the cloak around his neck, ensuring that the sword on his back is out of sight.

"Can we help you with something?" a guard asks as he approaches the gate.

"Yeah, we're here for Aedlin, we were supposed to travel together last night but plans changed at the last minute so we're running a little late."

"We weren't expecting anyone to be accompanying her."

"Oh, really?" Saviel asks, trying his best to sound surprised. "The King had given the guards a message last night to pass on at her arrival. You see, she doesn't travel anywhere without us. King Ulrich assigned us the job of protecting her some time ago."

The guard looks at Gerald with a raised eyebrow.

"Don't let his size fool you. He might be small, but he's as fast as they come."

The guard looks back at Saviel. "Listen, either way, absolutely no one is permitted into the castle until further notice."

"I'm sure you'll find that we are an exception to that rule."

"You'll find that no one is." the guard snaps, visibly running out of patience.

"Listen, we can turn back. I understand you just tried to do your job. But I need you to understand that we're just trying to do ours and if you're happy with us, returning to King Ulrich with word that." Saviel pauses and gives the guard a sympathetic smile. "What was your name?"

"Fallon, sir."

"Right. If you're happy with us returning to King Ulrich and having to inform him that you, Fallon, wouldn't allow us to do our job, then I suppose we should be on our way."

The guard looks back towards the castle then back at Saviel and Gerald, he bites his lip as he appears to consider what he should do.

Saviel makes a show out of picking the reigns back up.

"Thank you for your help." Saviel says with a friendly smile. Gerald smacks him on the leg to get his attention, then gives him a discreet, but confused shrug.

"Wait, wait. The guard calls after them. I'm going to regret this." He says, shaking his head as he proceeds to open the gate and let them in. "You can't take the carriage in; you will need to enter the grounds of the castle on foot."

"Sure thing." Saviel says and hops off the carriage. Gerald does the same and sticks to Saviel's side as they approach the gate.

"I don't suppose you could spare some food and water for them?" Saviel asks, pointing to the horses. "We struggled to find somewhere to stop for water in the dark.".

The guard hesitates for a moment before giving him a nervous smile.

"Sure, I'll see if I can sneak them round back to the stables for you."

"I appreciate it." Saviel says, then wastes no time crossing the castle grounds to its front entrance. To their surprise, the doors are already wide open and have been left entirely unguarded.

Gerald glances over at Saviel wearily, but they continue ahead into the castle. They barely cross the threshold when a woman with smudged makeup, unruly chestnut hair and a dishevelled dress stops as she crosses the room and glares at the both of them.

"No one is supposed to be here." Her voice is cold and uninviting.

"We are here to supervise Aedlin while she spends her

time here." Saviel says, trying his hardest to remain polite.

The woman's eyes flicker between Saviel and Gerald, and her entire body appears to begin trembling out of nowhere.

"Would you mind please directing us to her whereabouts? Then we will gladly leave you to continue on with whatever it is you were going. Perhaps you could even direct us to where we may find King Radaven or Queen Lulia?"

"You came here to Tarragor, a kingdom run for the last ten years by Queen Lulia and King Radaven. You enter their home uninvited; you ask to be told where you could find those who reside within its walls and yet, you don't even know the faces of the people whose home you've intruded on?"

"We are terribly sorry your highness, of course we know who you are, and we did not mean to intrude into your home, but we are already late, and King Khard would have our heads if we knew we had left Aedlin unaccompanied for so long." Gerald says with a nervous smile.

"Saviel, apologise to queen Lulia for your abruptness. It was awful rude of you to not even take the time to notice who you were talkin' to." Gerald gives Saviel a light nudge and Saviel clears his throat as he realises that Gerald is telling *him* who the woman in front of them is. How could he have known? She is in an awful state. The only clue that she is of some sort of stature is the quality of her dress, but even that is mud stained and wrinkled. For all he knew, it could have been stolen.

"I'm terribly sorry for the mistake. Please forgive me. It has been a long night and I'm awfully tired."

A wide smile that curls up at the edges and shows immaculate teeth spreads across Queen Lulia's face.

"You poor things do look tired. Come, why don't you follow me to the kitchen for a quick drink to freshen up a bit before I take you to see her?"

Saviel hesitates, her sudden change in mood in unnerving and something about her smile seems... off.

"Saviel, don't be rude. When a lady offers you a drink, you accept it, and you thank her."

Before Saviel can get the chance to say no, Gerald walks toward the Queen who, after giving Gerald one more smile, turns toward a door behind her. Gerald catches up to the queen and, with a defeated shake of his head, Saviel catches up to them both.

CHAPTER EIGHTEEN

Aedlin's head throbs and aches. Her arms and legs are stiff and her back feels like it's on fire. She blinks a few times to try to make out something, anything, in the dark. She cries out in pain as she pulls herself up from what feels like a damp path. Is she outside? She has to be. Maybe she was asleep, and it rained? She runs her hands over her dress. No, besides where she was laying, she's perfectly dry. She can't imagine that she would have chosen to fall asleep on the wet ground. Especially not in such a delicate gown, much less a gown that isn't hers, a gown that belongs to King Ulrich's sister. The same

King who sent her to Tarragor to meet with King Radaven and Queen Lulia. She rubs her eyes and tries again
to focus on what she can see. The air is still, even for a
calm night, it's *too* still. She reaches out to try to feel
around. Her fingertips connect with what feels like
bricks, she runs her hands along the length of it, she
reaches the end where she appears to come to a corner,
she continues to follow the bricks until her fingers touch
metal, metal she can wrap her hands around, multiple
bars that span the length of the bricks she had just followed.

"Oh no." she whispers as realisation sets in. She frantically shakes at the bars, blindly grabbing at one after
the other repeatedly, shaking each one to see if any will
give.

"Let me out!" she cries out in a panic.

There is no response from anyone, and the weight of
the situation drops her to her knees. She thinks back over
what happened when she arrived, meeting them, finding
out about the pregnancy, drinking the wine, feeling
wrong and then…. Her blade! She reaches for it but instead of feeling her boot or the handle of her blade she is
met with the bare skin of her foot.

She cries out, frustrated and this time, rather than being met with silence a pained groan comes from somewhere behind her.

"Who is that?" she says wearily as she slowly gets back to her feet and backs herself up against the bars. Whoever it is groans again but this time something about it sounds familiar.

She cautiously walks forward until her foot connects with something solid and warm on the ground.

She drops down beside whoever it is and asks them again who you are.

"Aedlin?" her heart is in her throat and panic sets back on with a fierceness.

"Saviel, Saviel you have to get up right now, come on." She pleads and tries to wrap her arms under his to gain leverage while trying to help him sit up.

"Aedlin?" he repeats, his voice becoming a little clearer.

"Yes, yes, it's me know you have to get up!"

He shifts his weight and tries to get up, but barely manages to move.

Aedlin tries once more to wrap her arms under his. With all the strength she can muster she manages to pull him up enough to allow him to lean on her.

She takes one of her arms out from under his and puts it on his face.

"Are you hurt?" she asks and moves his hair off his face.

"I don't think so, but I can't feel much of anything." He says in a broken whisper.

"What are you doing here?" she doesn't mean to yell, and the unexpected noise sounds odd in such an otherwise quiet place.

"We came here to find you."

We? What does he mean we? There is no one else here, she would have noticed by now.

"Saviel, who came here with you?"

He doesn't answer, so Aedlin lays him back down to see if she was wrong about them being the only ones in the cell.

She walks around the larger than she would have expected area, slowly, just as she had before when she was feeling around for Saviel.

She tries to keep track of what direction she is walking in, but struggles. Between the complete and utter darkness and still being groggy, she barely has a sense of direction.

"Saviel, no one else is here?" she calls out, to no response.

She turns back, hoping it's in the right direction, and

tries to find Saviel again. Before she can get to him a door opens close by to the cell, enough light floods in just enough to make out Saviel laying on the middle of the cell floor and against the one wall she hadn't walked by yet is a small shape, curled up into a ball. Under a mop of dark hair, the tip of a green ear pokes through.

"*Gerald.*" she whispers and runs over to him. She drops to her knees and turns him over.

She ignores the footsteps that approach the cell and takes advantage of the likely limited time that she will be able to see anything.

Once she rolls him onto his back, she puts her hand on his face to see if he would wake up. She gasps as soon as her fingers meet with his cold skin.

"You should make sure you say goodbye. I have no need to keep them here. I have guards coming to collect them within the hour, who will take them somewhere far enough from both here and Khard that no one will recognise their bodies."

"Why would you do this to them? You already had me. You didn't need to poison them or lock them in here and you certainly don't need to kill them!"

"And you didn't need to kill my husband when all he was trying to help me do was to ensure a prosperous and thriving home for our child."

"He poisoned me!"

"Oh please, it's hardly damaging. All you did was get almost a full night's sleep."

Aedlin walks to the cell door and stands directly in front of queen Lulia.

"Please, just let them go. They won't cause you any more harm than I already have."

"How much of a complete idiot do you take me for? Of course, they will cause me more trouble, they already lied their way through my front gate and into my home, the big one came with a sword hidden on his back, after what you did to my husband, I could hardly take the chance of risking my own and my baby's life."

"He is not some monster; he wouldn't hurt you or your baby! Neither of them would." Aedlin yells at the preposterousness of her implication.

"After the fight he put up and the way he wouldn't shut up or stop yelling your name as I was waiting for the wine to take effect, I wouldn't doubt a single thing that elf is capable of if it means saving you. And now, just like you did to me, I get to rip that away from you."

She walks back toward the door but stops before leaving through it.

"I hope you find your new home comfortable, although, I don' think you'll be needing to worry about staying in it for too long."

"What does that mean?"

"It means I thought the dark elf King would be interested to know that *someone* has been breading half-casts with the fae."

"No!" Aedlin cries out in horror as she feels for her necklace that isn't there.

"Don't waste your time trying anything stupid. Take this time you have left to say goodbye. You should consider yourself grateful that I too am not a monster and I'm still willing to at least offer you something you didn't give me the same decency for."

She slams the door shut behind her and Aedlin rushes straight back over to be by Gerald's side. She tries once more to touch his face, nothing.

"Gerald! Wake up!" she cries out, but he doesn't so much as twitch. She knows what she needs to do now, but every part of her wants to refuse. What if her instincts are right? She couldn't possibly handle knowing. She scoops up his head and runs her hands over her hair. Her tears begin to fall, and she cries out as she accepts what she is about to have to confirm.

She lowers her ear to his chest and holds her breath.

She stays there, waiting, giving his body the chance to show her that he is still there, just really unwell, but there is nothing. She continues to wait, pleading with him to wake up, then going silent again just in case she hears a single promising beat.

She lays his head back down and moves so she is positioned with her back against the wall. She scoops him back up and lets his head rest on her leg as she cries out for Saviel. She repeats his name more times than she can count. She cries, screams and cusses until she finally heard him stir.

"Saviel, I need you, you need to get up!" Aedlin pleads through tears. She holds Gerald tighter against her body.

"You're too cold, maybe that's all. Maybe I just need to help you get warm." She pulls as much of him as she can up against her and wraps as much of her arms around her as she can. She stays like this, silent besides the occasional hiccup from crying or the wince in pain from whatever it is that's wrong with her back until just a short while later a dim light from the sky outside begins to shine through a window too small and high up to be able to attempt to escape through.

Still, it lights the cell enough for her to be able to make out exactly where Saviel is in front of her, and the grey hue Gerald's skin has developed. She cries out again at the sight of him and runs her hand down along his side to try to re grip him and once more pull him closer. She notices something in his pocket as her hand runs over it. she reaches in and knows what it is as soon as she touches it.

She removes Fergus from his pocket and immediately, again, cries out.

"Aedlin!" Saviel calls out, surprised. He jumps up and is immediately by her side.

"What happened? What's wrong with him?"

Aedlin tries, but she can't get the words out. She can't bring herself to have to say it out loud. She can't understand why queen Lulia would do this to him. Why tell her that she plans to have them taken away to be killed while the whole time he was dead in here? She knows she is obviously deserving of having a heartbroken wife wanting to punish her for killing her husband, but killing Gerard is completely senseless.

"Aedlin, what happened?"

"I don't know. I came over to check on him after you started to wake up and he was so cold, I tried to find his heartbeat but... I... I couldn't find it."

"No!" Saviel shouts, making Aedlin startle.

"Where are we? We need to get him out of here.

Maybe there is still time to help him."

"It's too late, I don't know how long he had been gone for before I found him, and I've been sitting with him for too long."

"We have to try!" he shouts again but this time Aedlin ignores him, she brings Gerald closer to her face and plants a soft hiss on the top of his head then lays him back down on the ground.

"We don't have time for that now, we need to find a way to get you out of here before the guards come to re-trieve you."

"What are you talking about? We can't leave him here like this. He has to come with us? How could you think we would leave him alone?"

"I never said we would. I will be here with him. I said we need to find a way to get *you* out."

"No, no way. I'm not going anywhere without the both of you."

"You don't have a choice. She plans to have you killed. You need to get out of here before the guards come to retrieve you, or while the guards are here."

The door the Queen had entered through before slams open.

"Saviel, you need to do this. You need to run. As soon

as that cell door pushes past them and runs!" she pleads with him.

"Let's go. We don't have a lot of time." Someone with a low hood from the other side of the cell says before they mutter something under their breath.

The sound of the cell unlatching echoes off the surrounding walls.

"Who are you? Why are you helping us?" Saviel asks as he gets to his feet and positions himself between the stranger and Aedlin.

"Someone who doesn't have time for questions. Now let's go!"

Saviel picks up Gerald from the ground and walks through the open cell door. Aedlin hesitates, expecting this to be some kind of trap, but the muttering… she knows what that was.

"We aren't going anywhere until you tell me who you are."

The stranger lifts their hood to reveal their face and Aedlin almost loses the strength to stand at the sight of her.

"Seiche?"

"Yes, now let's go!"

This time Aedlin gladly listens and follows her and Saviel out of the cell, through the door, up a flight of stairs, through a long corridor that has multiple doors, one of which opens directly by the stables outside.

"We are going to get caught. There are guards everywhere."

"Not anymore, there isn't." she says coldly and continues to lead them toward a carriage with horses already attached.

"I'm sure King Ulrich would appreciate it if you retuned his horses to him." Seiche says, Aedlin is confused but brushes it off, it's not important right now, the only thing that important is getting as far away from here as possible, especially if queen Lulia was telling the truth and she really did send for King Erevin.

"I suspect you're right." Saviel says to Seiche as he lays Gerard into the carriage.

"Put these on." Seiche hands each of them a black robe. Once Aedlin and Saviel have put them on, she hands Saviel another.

"For your friend." She says with a sad smile. Saviel thanks her, then carefully lay the cloak over the top of Gerald.

"We will stop somewhere when we know we are safe to bury him before we get you both back to King Ulrich."

"No, I'm not going back until I do what I left that kingdom to do." Aedlin protests.

"Aedlin, please, we need to return together. You have injuries that need to be tended to, and the King needs to know that he sent you to an awaiting trap." Saviel says.

"The King already knows, that's how I knew you were here and why I came to get you." Seiche says as she grabs the horse's reigns.

"He sent me here knowing they were going to keep me as leverage?"

"No, of course not. He found out after you had all already left, one of her guards had overheard their plan and took it upon himself to travel to Khard, but unfortunately because you arrived early, he arrived late. Now I would love to continue this conversation with you, but we need to have it on the road."

Aedlin and Saviel join Seiche at the front of the carriage. It's cramped but wordlessly they both knew that neither of them wanted to be in the back with Gerald."

CHAPTER NINETEEN

Sweat beads form along Aedlin's hairline under the hood of her cloak. The blaring sun had been belting down on them for hours now. The abundance of trees surrounding them does little to offer relief under their cloaks. Aedlin grows more impatient and Seiche continues to refuse to tell either her or Saviel where they are going. All Aedlin knows, thanks to Saviel questioning Seiche, is that this is not the way back to Khard.

"I'm grateful for you saving us, but this is getting ridiculous. We have been travelling, in the open, in the heat, without water for hours. The least you can do is tell us where we are going." Saviel says through what sounds to be gritted teeth.

"We will stop just up ahead. There is a small river where we can stop to hydrate."

They continue on for another thirty minutes or so in silence before the sound of rushing water breaks through the trees ahead. Aedlin fights the urge to jump down from the carriage and sprint the rest of the way to the inviting water.

Seiche gets the horses to stop as soon as they reach the bank of the river. They all get down from the carriage and Saviel and Aedlin immediately rush to the bed of the rover, drop to their knees and scoop the water up in their hands, and over and over again gulp it down. Only after the eighth gulp does Aedlin look up and notice that Seiche has not joined them, instead she is looking over the horses while they drink.

"It's time for the two of you to say your final good-byes to your friend. We can't take him much further from here without risking getting stopped. Having a body in your carriage is hard enough to explain yourself out of. Add that to the risk we are already taking with Aedlin not having anything to shield her identity."

Aedlin instinctively pulls her hood further over and

lowers her head. The inevitable had to happen eventually, but if they do this it means acceptance, it means finding his home, his family, and having the decency to tell them what has happened.

"We need wood and something to bind it together with." Aedlin says, continuing to pat the horse.

"What for?" Saviel asks, confused.

"Aedlin, that tradition is for the fae royal line. It's a tradition that is thousands of years old."

"It's Queen Aedlin, and that goblin died trying to rescue me for the second time. I don't care if it is a tradition for only the royal bloodline. None of them have ever been more deserving of such a send-off than him. I have not had the opportunity to make a single decision as queen yet, so let this be my first. I am a childless queen of the throne who has no born heir. I am gladly giving the title of heir to Gerald if that means I can give him the damn funeral he deserves."

"What do you mean, Queen?" Saviel asks with wide eyes.

Seiche throws Aedlin a warning glance, but she is bone tired, tired of running, tired of being scared and tired of not taking charge of a single thing that has happened to her or her kingdom. She never should have needed to be rescued, she never should have left her kingdom and she never should have trusted anyone when her gut was telling her otherwise.

She removes her hood, then her cloak altogether. She's tired of the secrets and from this point on, she will no longer hide behind them.

"I am Queen Aedlin of Malheim, I am the carer, protector and mother of all fae-folk and protector of the elder tree, and I will not wait any longer to do the decent thing and send off our friend like he deserves."

"Do you know what you're risking by doing this?" Seiche snaps at her.

"Everything, and it's about time we do. The time for running and hiding died with me, mother."

Seiche shakes her head at Aedlin but chooses to not say anything else and, to Aedlin's dismay, Saviel leaves.

"You know by the end of the week, multiple kingdoms, including Withhhorn, will know about you and Malheim."

"He wouldn't, but even if he does, let them come, let them learn of the awesome power fae kind is *actually* capable of when they are given permission to use it."

"I'm not going anywhere, nor am I going to betray Aedlin. Sorry, Queen Aedlin, in such a way. She asked for wood, so I'm gathering wood."

Saviel drops the few logs he has already found and leaves to go find more. This time Aedlin joins him, giving herself the opportunity to both step away from the tension building between her and Seiche and to hopefully have a moment to talk with Saviel.

"Thank you for coming to get me." Aedlin says quietly as she catches up to Saviel.

"You're welcome." He says, but keeps his gaze forward.

"Saviel, I'm sorry I didn't tell you."

"You didn't lose your memory on that cliff, did you?"

Aedlin stops walking. "No."

Saviel stops too and pauses, appearing to think over his next question. "The fae, they are all there, aren't they? In that forest?"

"Yes, Malheim is hidden within the forbidden Forest."

"I see."

"Saviel, I couldn't tell you, you have to believe that I wanted to, but it wasn't safe. When I left, Malheim was already under attack. The reason I had to find Seiche was because she was the only one who could help. She used magic to protect Malheim, but if I returned before being told it was safe to do so I would have risked everyone's lives. Malheim's location has been kept secret since my mother was young. I thought keeping it that way was what was for the best."

Saviel approaches Aedlin. His expression gives nothing away, and it makes her feel uneasy.

"Aedlin, relax. I'm not mad. I understand. It's just, it's a lot to take in, especially right now when we are about to have a funeral for Gerald. So, if you don't mind, fir right now can we just focus on one thing at a time, which should start with Gerald?"

"Yes, of course we can." Aedlin says as she relaxes her shoulders.

Saviel plants a kiss on the top of her head. He stays they for a few seconds then backs away and continues looking for more wood.

Aedlin decides to try a different direction. She only gets a few feet away when she notices something has been dug up and it looks like it has been cut in half. She kneels down to get a closer look. It's big enough to be the trunk of a tree–the elder tree. She has found one of the roots of the elder tree that have been destroyed. She reaches down and runs her hand along it. A sharp static travels throughout her fingers and she quickly pulls away and shakes her hand.

"What the?" the part of the root she touched slowly

changes from dark and limp to light.

She reaches down to touch it again, this time with both hands. A familiar tingling feeling returns, the same one from when she had to attack King Radaven, just the same as when she attacked the guys in the tavern. But this time the feeling doesn't stay just in her hands. The longer she continues to touch the root of the tree, the more it travels, from her arms, through to her chest.

The tree root continues to change colour, and it grows and stretches, reconnecting itself to its broken half. She quickly realises what is happening and moves her left hand to the other side of the broken root.

"Seiche, come quickly! She calls out and immediately she can hear her running toward Aedlin.

"Oh, my word!" Seiche exclaims in disbelief.

"Are you alright? What's happening?" Saviel asks as he gets closer to them.

"She's fine, don't touch her!" Seiche shouts as Saviel approaches.

The tree root continues to brighten and stretch until eventually it reconnects and there is no sign that her father or his men had ever touched it.

"I don't believe it." Seiche whispers.

"I fixed it. I bought it back to life. How is that possible? A week ago, I didn't have *any* magic within me. Now I'm capable of this?"

"I think you'll find it was always within you." Seiche responds but sounds distracted.

"I can end this; I can heal the roots of the elder tree and give magic back to those who remain. I can."

Aedlin trails off and gets to her feet. She sprints back towards the river, throws the door of the carriage open and places her hands on Gerald's body. She wills for that feeling in her hands to return.

"Please, please just let this work.

"Aedlin no!" Seiche yells and wraps her hands around Aedlin's waist and tries to pull her away.

"Get off me!" Aedlin waves one her hands back behind her. This time that feeling is back and Seiche flies back as the force from Aedlin's magic connects with her.

"Aedlin, what did you do?" Saviel yells as he rushes to make sure Seiche is okay.

"I can save him, I have to!" she cries.

She continues to hold her hands on his chest. She wills the feeling back. She thinks of the tree root, King Ulrich, and the tavern. It starts to happen, but it's faint and only in the tips of her fingers.

"Get her away from him now, you can't let her bring him back!" Seiche screams.

Saviel does as Seiche says. He traps Aedlin's arms under his and picks her up. she cries out and kicks as hard as she can, but he doesn't let up. her back is screaming at her in pain, but she ignores it. She tries biting him. He cries out in pain but keeps his grip tight.

"Take her back to the tree root and don't let her go until I come get you."

"I'm so sorry." Saviel whispers in her ear as he carries her away from Gerald and Seiche.

"Take me back! Why won't you let me save him? I can fix him!" She continues to yell, kick, and struggle against him.

They make it back to the tree root and he continues to hold her in place.

"Aedlin, please stop fighting me."

"No! why would you listen to her?" she cries. "Why don't you want me to bring him back?"

"Of course I wish for him to be back, but not like this. You can't just bring someone back from the dead Aedlin. You're not thinking clearly."

The sound of horse's hooves approaches them, and they both look up to see Seiche sitting at the front of the carriage. She gets down and opens the door of the carriage that is now empty. Aedlin screams through the tears that stain her face.

"What did you do?" she shouts.

"Get her in the carriage."

"I'm not sure if…" Saviel tries to say, but Seiche cuts him off.

"Now!"

He does as Seiche says and carries Aedlin toward the carriage. She tries digging her heels into the ground, but it does nothing.

"Saviel please." She cries and stops fighting.

He loosens his grip on her. It's not enough for her to break free but it's enough for Seiche to notice.

"Oh, for goodness' sake." Seiche leaves the door of the carriage where she was waiting and comes to stand by Aedlin.

"What did you do? She repeats. This time she doesn't scream or shout. It's more of a broken whimper and the sound of it makes Saviel loosen his grip more.

"What I had to do? You wanted him in the river, that's where he went."

Aedlin's mouth falls open and her hands begin to tingle.

"You just dumped him?"

"No, of course not. I'm not heartless."

Aedlin manages to wriggle one of her hands free. In a blink she tries to reach touch Seiche, hoping that this time she will do a little more than make her fall back. But before she can, Seiche moves out of the way, then grabs Aedlin's chin and tips her face back.

"Don't be a fool." She warns Saviel before tipping a small glass bottle of liquid town Aedlin's throat.

"Get away from her!" Saviel yells. He lets go of Aedlin, rips the bottle from Seiche's hand.

"What did you give her?" he demands.

"Something to help her sleep until we get back to Khard. Now get her into the damn carriage like I asked."

"She isn't going anywhere with you. Neither of us are."

"Yes, you are. You will both return to Khard because she made a promise to return, and I made a promise to ensure that happens.

"A promise to who?" Saviel asks.

"To her future husband."

CHAPTER TWENTY

Aedlin's head is pounding, and her stomach is a churning mess. She can feel someone's arms around her and the sound of the horse's feet smacking against the path outside. Whoever is holding her tightens their grip and pulls her in closer to their chest. The familiar smell of leather and soap fill the air and she breathes a sigh of relief.

"Stay quiet." Saviel whispers right by her ear.

The memory of what happened comes flooding back at the sound of his voice and she shoves herself out of his arms.

He doesn't try to stop her, but she can see that he is

worried.

"You stay the hell away from me!" she whispers through clenched teeth.

"Aedlin, I'm so sorry. I know you're pissed and probably feeling betrayed again by me. But right now, I need you to trust me, just one more time, even if it's the last time you ever do. Because I'm going to get you out of here and away from her."

Aedlin scoffs at him and tries to move back further, but her back was barely an inch away from the wall of the carriage as it is.

"I don't need your help. As soon as I make Seiche stop, the both of us are getting out of this carriage and going our own separate ways. You go can home to Khard or wherever you decide to run away to next and I will go where I need to be. Without you."

For the longest time he doesn't say anything, he just stares at her. It feels like he is waiting for her to try something, anything, but instead they are stuck in a stale—mate with each other.

"She plans to take you back to King Ulrich." Saviel finally says, but for some reason he can't seem to look at her.

"I'm not surprised. That's where she wanted me to be from the very beginning. It would make sense that she would want me to return to him. Not that it's any longer a concern of yours."

"Do you know why she wants you back there with him?" he asks slowly.

Aedlin's heart rate picks up as a mixture of panic and anger sets in. He helped Seiche, he wouldn't let her even try to bring back Gerald. How could she ever look at him again? How could she ever trust him again when in a single moment he betrayed her by choosing to listen to Seiche? Someone he doesn't even know.

"It doesn't matter why. What matters is why you would listen to her. Why would you not allow yourself to see that I was doing the right thing for Gerald? He didn't deserve to be killed. I'm the reason he was, so of course I should have bought him back *if* I had of been able to."

"I listened to her because you're not supposed to come back once you're gone, Aedlin. It's unnatural."

"No one knows for absolute sure." She scoffs, making Saviel roll his eyes.

"Aedlin." His voice is low and something about it catches her attention.

"What?"

"I need to know if you know why she is taking you

back to King Ulrich."

"I told you; she wanted me in Khard for my safety. Why do you keep asking?"

He runs his hands through his hair and lets out a frustrated groan.

"Why do you keep avoiding answering me properly? I didn't ask about you going to Khard. I asked about her taking you back to King Ulrich. Now, do you know why?"

"He had mentioned something about being asked to keep me safe in the castle." She shrugs, she answers slowly, carefully, wanting to tread lightly to see if he is trying to gage the answer she suspects he is looking for from her.

"Do you know that she is taking you back to him so the two of you can be married?" there is hope in his voice and she knows he is waiting for her to say no. Part of her wants to. She owes him nothing, not anymore, not even the truth. But the elf sitting in front of her who is leaning forward in his seat anticipating her answer, the elf whose eyes are desperate to hear the answer the answer he is looking for. Is the same elf who she spent the last days being vulnerable with, eating with, laughing with and just as she pleaded with him to remember the version of her who he got to know, she wants to give him the same. So she gives him the answer she knows will hurt, but it's the one he deserves.

"I didn't know why was taking me back because of that, but yes, King Ulrich told me this morning that our parents had planned for us to marry."

"And you agreed? Hours after I confessed to you how I felt you agreed to marry another man?"

"It's not that simple, and yes, I agreed to it, but I never had any intention of *actually* going through with it. I only agreed, so *he* would agree to let me leave to find my father."

The carriage slows, and Aedlin looks out of the window of the cart. They are approaching Khard already. She's left it too late. She either has to get out now or not at all.

"We are almost at Khard. I can't allow her to make it all the way there with me still in this cart. I still need to locate my father; I need to heal more of the elder tree roots, and I need to go home."

Saviel looks around frantically, as if he is trying to figure out what to do or say. He halts.

"What if you start off small, start with healing the tree roots, help magic using folk all across Agoura regain strength in their magic, there may only be few left but there will still be enough who would be willing to help you face your father? You stand more of a chance of walking away from him alive if you accept and allow help. From there, we can figure the rest out. I will help you figure the rest out."

Aedlin shakes her head in disbelief.

"Saviel, it's not as simple as that. Locating the roots alone across all of Agoura is an almost impossible task that I will take a countless amount of time. I need to start by putting an end to my father, killing more roots and magic users."

"king Ulrich has a map of the elder tree's roots. It starts from the forest where you woke up. The elder tree is somewhere in there. The roots expand across the entirety of Agoura, but if we know the location of the roots, we can get it done."

"How do you know that?"

"When the guards took us to the castle, for some reason they decided to unhook the horses and take us in through a side entrance. Gerald and I noticed the enormous map on the wall in a room with its door open as we passed. Gerald asked what it was, and the guard told him."

Aedlin considers Saviel's proposition, her walls are back up more than they ever were with him now, and she's not sure if they will ever completely come back down so if she does agree to what she knows is right, which is she's better and safer with him, then clear boundaries will need to be set. Her priorities begin with her father and very close to that is her return to Malheim, but he has a point. They will be stronger with numbers. Perhaps those numbers can include fae, assuming they are all alright. Melody is sure to be against it and that is something she will have to prepare herself for, but there are hundreds of fae who would be willing to help.

"Alright, we will return to Malheim. We will make a copy of the map and as soon as possible we will begin bringing magic back to Malheim."

Saviel just nods. Aedlin isn't sure what to make of his nonresponse, but she lets it go and watches out of the window as they approach King Ulrich's castle.

"Aedlin." Saviel whispers and once again struggles to look at her.

"What is it?"

"I know this isn't going to mean much of anything to you right now, or maybe even ever, but I need you to know that I truly am sorry for everything that happened earlier. I'm not sorry for stopping you from trying to bring *him* back. But I am sorry for how I had to do it."

His soft pleading words pull at everything inside her that had already decided it wants to accept that he wanted to be with her. She had felt close to others before, of course. But never anything like this. The feeling she got when she is with Saviel and new and exciting and make her wants to do mushy things like, continue traveling, but for fun instead of survival, she wants picnics on the shore and reding next to each other, quietly sipping tea at the end of a busy day.

"You're right, I can't forgive you, not yet, but I will." Aedlin reaches forward and grasps Saviel's hand in hers. She squeezes his hand, and his shoulders relax as he drops his head low.

After a few seconds he lifts his head back up and this time, he looks right at her.

"I look forward to the day, no matter how far away that might be." He is quiet for a moment, but Aedlin can see that he wants to say something else.

"What is it?"

"Does this mean you will let me come with you to heal the roots of the elder tree?"

"It would be stupid of me to not have you with me. What sort of damsel would I be without a big strong elf by my side to ensure my safety?"

She lets go of Saviel's hand and leans back against the wall of the carriage with a smug smile.

"I've had the pleasure of seeing you handle your

blade. Your nerves have you at risk of being sloppy, but when you need to be, you're quick on your feet and you, when it mattered more, you didn't hesitate. I don't encourage the killing of many, not even the elf king's men, but it's good to know you can hold your own when needed."

Aedlin shakes her head and nervously rubs her hands together. The plan sounded perfect, but even with all of her training form Melody, she is in over her head. Every step of the way since her mother died, she has made mistake after mistake. Her first one was not allowing Melody to drive her sword's blade through Dareyth's chest. All of this could have been avoided if someone had done something sooner like give the unused dungeons a reason to have been built- besides as a hidden escape route.

"Saviel, I froze when I stabbed that guard, and before you bring it up, every time, except one, that I have used my magic so far has been an accident, or at the very least, something I have no control over."

"I'm happy to help you work on it."

"Saviel, we don't have the time for me to figure out how to use magic. I only just discovered I have or how to not be pearlized by shock after I kill someone."

"We will make the time. We have to in order to make

this work. You want your father to answer for the atrocities he has committed, right?"

"Yes?"

"Well, this might not exactly come as a shock to you, given how you know what happened to my family, but I would also like to live to see the end of his reign. No matter what that ends up looking like. And if that happens to end up looking like death at your hand, you need to be ready for that. You won't have the opportunity to freeze up with him. He won't give you that opportunity, so you can't give it to him."

"Okay, you're right. We'll make the time." Aedlin says quietly.

The carriage stops suddenly at Aedlin, looks out the small window and cusses under her breath at the sight of the guards who are approaching the carriage.

"Don't let them out yet. I need to speak with the King first." Seiche says from somewhere beside the cart.

"We need to ensure that Aedlin is safe and unharmed." One of the guards says, she recognises him as the one who showed her back to her room the night she ate dinner with King Ulrich.

Aedlin reaches out to open the door of the carriage, but Saviel pushes her hand away.

"Not yet. It sounded like she suspected you would be out for much longer than you were. I think we should let her think you still are, just so we can figure out what she is up to get the upper hand." He whispers.

Aedlin nods in agreeance and Saviel gets back down on the floor of the cart.

"Quickly!" he whispers and motions for her to get back on the floor.

She makes sure she is careful to not let herself be seen moving through the window and joins Saviel on the cramped floor.

He pulls her into his arms, and she looks up at him with raised eyebrows.

"It's going to be more believable." He shrugs.

She allows herself to sink into his arms and rests her head against his chest. She closes her eyes listens out for Seiche and the guards.

"Very well, feel free to check for yourself. She's perfectly fine."

Aedlin hears someone open the door and feels Saviel tense. He tightens his grip on her and she realises that is must be Seiche who opened the door.

"Tell them she's sleeping." Seiche whispers through her teeth.

Saviel doesn't say anything back to her, but Aedlin feels Saviel move and a low growl hum in his chest.

"See, she's fine, just tired, as I'm sure can be expected."

"Why are her clothes so dirty and torn?"

She was poisoned and locked in a dungeon. What do you expect?"

"Hmm." The guard responds, sounding unsure. "Very well." His words come out slowly.

"Go find King Ulrich. Tell him Aedlin has been returned." The guard says.

"Right away." Someone responds and their footsteps quickly recede.

The door closes and Saviel readjusts his grip around Aedlin, she takes the small, quiet moment they have to enjoy the feel of being so close to him, the warmth between them takes her right back to their kiss and she fights with everything within herself to not open her eyes, wrap her arms around his neck and pull him close to her.

"Why has Aedlin not been bought inside? If she is so tired, let her rest in a bed for heaven's sake?" King Ulrich shouts angrily.

"She can be taken inside soon, but first, there's something I need to discuss with you."

"What is it, Seiche?" King Ulrich replies, sounding distracted.

"It's about Aedlin's mother, Frayett."

Aedlin stiffens at the sound of her mother's name. She hasn't had to hear it since she left, and she hadn't realised how much something as simple as hearing her name would hurt.

"She's alive." Seiche says, making her voice low but Aedlin can still hear her clearer than ever. She sits up and tries to scramble to her feet.

"She's with King Erevin." Seiche continues.

Aedlin's vision blurs and the world around her is moving faster than she can keep up. Her stomach churns so hard it hurts. She slams the door of the carriage open. King Ulrich's eyes widen at the sight of her.

This isn't possible. Her mother is dead. She sat by her bedside as she took her final breath. She did everything she could to protect Malheim and Aedlin from being found by her father. Why would she fake her death and return to him? *How* could she return to him after everything he had done?

"Aedlin?" King Ulrich asks and steps toward her.

"I need your map of the elder tree roots and every guard you can spare."

"What, why?" King Ulrich asks as he reaches out a hand to help her out of the carriage but she waves him away.

"Because we have work to do." Aedlin says as she brushes past Seiche and makes her way up the stairs of King Ulrich's castle.

ABOUT THE AUTHOR

J. A. Garth is an author from Qld Australia who has a passion for fantasy novels that get you lost in another world, crime thrillers that keep you on the edge of your seat and dark romances that make you quiver. Born in 1996 with a love for reading for about that same amount of time. She has dreamt of joining her Author hero's since she was a little girl. After moving to Qld from Victoria at 16, she worked various jobs including cleaning and being a barista/waitress. By the time she was 23 she was married, had her three children and published her first novel.

When she isn't working on a new project, she enjoys resting with a good book, watching sitcoms, true crime documentaries or alien conspiracies. And expanding her sometimes good, but most of the time not so good, cooking skills.

www.ingramcontent.com/pod-product-compliance
Lightning Source LLC
Chambersburg PA
CBHW030605120726
47904CB00006B/1783